"I don't want your gratitude."

Brad's tone had hardened again.

"Well, you're getting it regardless." There was an ineradicable tremor in Kerry's voice. "Why does it always have to finish up like this between us?"

A breath of wind stirred the glowing embers, the sudden leap of flame highlighting taut features. "Because you're driving me crazy," he said. "Because I had my life all mapped out before you came back on the scene. Because you're who you are, and I'm who I am."

She said huskily, "I'm not sure what that's supposed to mean."

He turned his head to look at her then, the firelight flickering in his eyes. "It means that we're as incompatible as they come."

KAY THORPE, an English author, has always been able to spin a good yarn. In fact, her teachers said she was the best storyteller in the school—particularly with excuses for being late! Kay then explored a few unsatisfactory career paths before giving rein to her imagination and hitting the jackpot with her first romance novel. After a roundabout route, she'd found her niche at last. The author is married with one son.

Books by Presents

Don't miss any of our special offers. Write to us at the following address for information on our newest releases.

Harlequin Reader Service
P.O. Box 1397, Buffalo, NY 14240
Canadian address: P.O. Box 603,
Fort Erie, Ont. L2A 5X3

KAY THORPE

against all odds

Harlequin Books

TORONTO • NEW YORK • LONDON
AMSTERDAM • PARIS • SYDNEY • HAMBURG
STOCKHOLM • ATHENS • TOKYO • MILAN

Harlequin Presents first edition April 1991
ISBN 0-373-11356-0

Original hardcover edition published in 1990
by Mills & Boon Limited

AGAINST ALL ODDS

CHAPTER ONE

THE Monterrey flight was already boarding, Kerry noted, glancing up at the departure display as they came through into the main concourse. Providing her connection to Las Meridas was also on time, she should reach her destination by nightfall.

'I still find it difficult to see you as an engineer,' confessed the man at her side, taking in the smooth oval of her face, the heavy fall of red-gold hair. 'You just don't look the type!'

'Looks aren't everything,' she responded. 'Anyway, the degree is only half the battle. I still have a long way to go before I can even think about becoming chartered.'

'These next few weeks should be good experience, at least,' he said. 'It's an opportunity most trainees would give their eye-teeth for.'

'I know.' She pulled a humorous face. 'I suppose it gives me an unfair advantage over my fellow graduates having a top consultant for a father.'

'I doubt if many would lose any sleep over it if the positions were reversed.'

'Probably not. I was just paying lip service.' She held out a hand. 'Thanks for the hospitality, Robert. And thank Celia again for me, too, will you, please?'

'Only too sorry you couldn't stay longer,' he returned. 'Although I realise you must be eager to get started. Of course, you're not actually on the workforce, are you?'

'Not as such, no,' she acknowledged. 'The contract's too near completion for any formal appointment. I'm there to observe and imbibe—and set a precedent for the future, I hope. Women are still comparative rarities in civil engineering.'

'At the risk of repeating myself, particularly ones who look the way you do.' His smile acknowledged her grimace. 'It's been some time since I saw John, but there's little resemblance.'

'I'm supposed to take after my mother,' she said. 'You met her, didn't you?'

'Only the once, and that very briefly. Sad that she had to go so young.'

'Yes.' Never having known the mother who had died giving birth to her, Kerry felt no more than a fleeting pang. 'Dad should have married again.'

'For some men there's only one woman,' came the response.

'I don't really believe——' she began, then broke off, stomach muscles contracting as her glance lit on the dark-haired man moving through the crowd some short distance away. He had his back to them, but there was no mistaking that breadth of shoulder, the leanness of hip, the height which set him head and shoulders above most others in his vicinity. What would Brad Halston be doing in Mexico City? The last she had heard of him he had been working on a job in Algeria.

'Kerry?' Robert Baseheart was looking at her oddly. 'Is something wrong?'

She gave herself a mental shake as the man vanished into the throng. A passing resemblance, that was all. 'Sorry, I thought I saw someone I knew. I'd better be going on through.'

'Take care,' he said at the barrier. 'That's rough country up there in the Sierras.'

Most passengers were already on board the 737 when she eventually reached the gate. Her seat was near the front of the cabin on the aisle side. Even as she settled herself and reached for her seatbelt, the stewardess was closing the main door.

They were due in Monterrey by early afternoon, giving her an hour or so on the ground between flights. Alan Pope knew she was coming, of course, but not the exact date, so she would have to make her own way up to the dam site. That shouldn't prove too difficult. There must be a fairly regular flow of traffic.

Take-off was smooth. Kerry left her seatbelt fastened when the illuminated signs went out and reached for the flight magazine tucked into the pocket in front of her. She murmured a polite refusal when the man next to her asked if she would like a drink, keeping her eyes on the printed page and hoping he wouldn't try to start a conversation. She wasn't in the mood for idle chat.

After one or two further overtures, he appeared to take the hint. Finishing the magazine, she took her copy of Hind's *Engineering For Dams* out of her carry-on bag. Since flying was always boring, she might as well take advantage of the time to do some studying. She was certainly going to need it.

Persuading her father to send her out to Mexico for some initial practical experience hadn't in the end proved as difficult as she had anticipated. She wanted to specialise as he had chosen to specialise: dams and bridges—every one a different kind of challenge. The Meridas was within a few weeks of completion, but she could still learn plenty. Next time she would want to see a job through from the very beginning.

His pleasure when she had first announced her intention of taking a civil engineering degree course had known no bounds. He had given her every encouragement. As she had told Robert Baseheart, she still had a lot of ground to cover before she could call herself truly qualified, but she intended leaving no stone unturned in her efforts to follow in her father's footsteps. One day in the not too distant future she could be resident engineer in charge of a project herself. That was something worth working towards.

How she was going to reconcile that future with her relationship with Tim Linacre was something she didn't care to think about too hard. If she achieved her ambitions, marriage between them would be a series of hellos and goodbyes. Could love survive under such circumstances?

Was what she felt for Tim the right kind of love, anyway? came the thought, hastily pushed to the back of her mind. These next weeks apart would help sort things out.

The morning wore on. By the time an early lunch had been served and eaten, and the trays cleared away, they were nearing journey's end.

The toilets were at the rear of the cabin. Making her way aft, Kerry felt the breath catch again in her throat as her eyes fell on the man occupying a window seat some dozen rows back. No doubt about it this time. That lean, hardbitten face was etched too deeply on her inner mind.

He was looking out through the port, apparently absorbed in the landscape far below. Open at the throat, his shirt revealed a triangle of dark hair, bringing a quiver of memory to stir her senses. Brad Halston: brilliant engineer, total louse! At least he had been four years ago.

He would be thirty-four now, she reckoned, forcing herself to move on. Perhaps even married. No concern of hers, anyway. He was in the past. Let him stay there.

Except that his presence here on this flight elicited a certain question. True, Monterrey was a long way from Las Meridas, and there had to be other projects in which he could be involved, but the coincidence still troubled her. His firm specialised in dam construction, too; that fact alone brought the odds down. How many other dams were being built in this part of the world?

On the other hand, her father would surely have mentioned it if KDC was the construction company handling this job? Always providing he even remembered she'd ever met Brad, came the immediate rider. He certainly hadn't known about their brief association; she hadn't wanted him to know. Although he had always tended to let her go her own way, she had suspected that even he might have frowned on any serious relationship with a man twelve years older.

Brad was still gazing through the port when she returned to her seat. Short of sitting down in the empty seat beside him and asking his destination, she could do nothing but hope she was wrong in her assumption. The last thing she wanted was to have to face him again.

She made sure of being one of the first off the plane at the terminal, losing herself in the crowds thronging the concourse. The flight to Las Meridas was with one of the small domestic airlines. Having scarcely touched her lunch, she supposed she should think about finding something to eat now. This might be her only chance of a meal before reaching her destination.

She settled in the end for coffee and *tortillas* in the snack bar, ignoring the efforts of a nearby group of young men to attract her attention. Her looks were sometimes more of a hindrance than a help, she admitted. Even her father's old friend had been unable to take her aims all that seriously. But she'd show the doubting Thomases. She'd show them all! Brains weren't the prerogative of the plain.

There were perhaps a dozen other people already waiting in the cramped area which constituted the airline's departure lobby when she got there. Of Brad Halston there was no sign. In all probability she had been worrying over nothing. Pure coincidence, that was all. Not that it was going to be all that easy to put the incident aside. Just seeing him again had brought back memories she preferred to forget.

The plane on which they were to travel was an ancient twin-engined affair which looked ready for the scrap heap. Passenger seating was limited to no more than a couple of dozen all told, she found when they eventually boarded, the rest of the space having been turned over to cargo transport. The distinctly grubby state of the upholstery made her glad she had chosen to wear her oldest and most comfortable cotton trouser suit. Khaki showed few marks.

With the pilot already at the controls, there appeared to be some delay. One more passenger was still to come, Kerry gathered. It was with a sinking heart that she saw the tall figure emerge from the building just vacated. No mere coincidence, after all. They had to be heading for the same place. And how did she deal with that situation?

By facing it out, came the immediate response. By not allowing him to see she was in any way affected by his presence. She didn't really have a choice. If he was with the construction team they were going to be running into each other quite a lot during the coming weeks.

He came on up the steps of the plane with the lithe and easy movement she recalled so well. Seated two rows back, she braced herself to meet the grey eyes as they came to rest on her face, even managing a cool little nod of acknowledgement.

That Brad hadn't been aware of her presence on the plane was obvious from the fleeting expression which crossed his features, the sudden compression about the well-cut mouth. Then he was moving forwards, bending to ask the man sitting next to her if he would mind exchanging seats with him; sliding in beside her with a look that hardly needed words.

'What the devil are you doing here?' he demanded.

'The same thing you are, I assume,' she responded smoothly. 'I'm on my way to the Meridas dam site.'

One dark brow lifted. 'To do what?'

'Join my father's team. He's project consultant.'

'I know damn well he's project consultant. That doesn't answer the question.'

'I got my degree last month,' she said. 'I'm here to gain some site experience.'

'Is that a fact?'

'Yes, it is.' She was fighting to stay on top of her inclinations. 'I'm sorry if the idea doesn't meet with your approval, but that's your tough luck!'

They were moving out on to the runway now, lining up to await take-off instructions from the tower. He studied her without speaking for a moment or two, the appraisal cool and calculated. 'You came in via Houston?' he asked obliquely.

Kerry shook her head. 'I came up from Mexico City this morning.' She registered his surprise with some faint satisfaction. 'I saw you on the plane.'

'So why didn't you make yourself known?'

Her shrug was as indifferent as she could make it. 'Why bother?'

'Scared of facing me?' His voice had a sardonic edge. 'So you damned well should be!'

Green eyes flashed. 'You can't say it wasn't merited!'

'How's that?'

'You don't need it spelled out for you,' she said bitterly. 'You knew exactly how I felt about you.'

'I knew how you thought you felt about me. Eighteen-year-old girls often imagine themselves in love with older men.'

'Not without encouragement, and you gave me plenty of that!'

A muscle tautened fleetingly at the point of his jaw. 'I may have given you some, I admit. You were pretty hard to resist.'

'But you managed well enough in the end.'

'Let's just say I wasn't ready to tie myself down at that point.' He paused, his mouth taking on an added slant. 'You got your revenge.'

Kerry bit her lip. 'You asked for it.'

'So you keep telling me.' He made a sudden, impatient gesture. 'Beside the point, anyway. To get back to the original subject, there's no way you're going up on site.'

She stared at him. 'You hardly have the authority to stop me!'

'As project manager, I have the authority to do whatever I see fit regarding site operation,' he returned hardily. 'This plane comes back to Monterrey in the morning. You'd better take it.'

It took a real effort to keep her tone level. 'Still favouring the closed shop?'

His shrug was brief. 'Women engineers may be on the up and up, but in jobs like this one, stuck miles from anywhere, sex is always going to be a problem. Unless she's willing to take on some occupational therapy out of hours, that is.'

'With the project manager at the head of the list, I suppose!'

Mockery infiltrated his regard. 'That would depend on the woman. I might not fancy her.'

'The shoe might even be on the other foot,' she retorted. 'Contrary to your own undoubted opinion, Brad, you're not irresistible!'

The mockery increased. '*Now* she tells me!'

Kerry closed her eyes as the plane began its run, bracing herself against the shuddering of the fuselage with the very real fear that there might not be any problem to overcome should this aircraft do what it was threatening to do and shake itself to pieces. There was a point at which she was sure it wasn't even going to lift off the ground, but then there came the sudden smoothing out of sound and motion, and she opened her eyes again to see the concrete falling away beneath them.

Brad had his head back against the rest. He looked completely relaxed. She allowed her gaze to drift down the hard, lean length of him—recalling how it had felt to be held close to him. From the moment her father had introduced them that day, younger men had faded into insignificance for her.

She had gone to the office to drag her father out to lunch, eager to tell him her A-level results face to face— to see his expression when she announced her plans for the future. His secretary had said he had someone with

him, but it hadn't made any difference. She'd gone
breezing right in . . .

John Wallace looked round from the drawings pinned
to the drawing-board with a frown which swiftly turned
to a smile when he saw his daughter standing in the
doorway.

'Good news?' he asked.

Eyes bright, Kerry nodded. 'Straight As!'

'Congratulations,' proffered the man at her father's
side, drawing her attention for the first time. He had his
back to the window, tanned features clearly outlined,
the brown suede jacket emphasising the breadth of his
shoulders. Six feet two at least, Kerry judged in that first
breathless moment of awareness.

'Thanks,' she said.

'This is Brad Halston,' her father supplied. 'He's with
KDC Construction. My daughter, Brad.'

The latter's smile made her heart flutter. 'Hi.'

'Hello.' She searched her mind for some intelligent
remark to add. 'Dams, isn't it? Must be the Saudi job.'

'That's right.' The smile came again. 'Not just a pretty
face!'

'You disappoint me, Mr Halston,' she responded
blandly, recovering her normal poise. 'I'd have expected
something a little more original.'

One eyebrow lifted, amusement mingled with something else not so easily defined as he studied her. 'Lazy
of me,' he agreed.

'You're forgiven.' Her skin was tingling as if he had
reached out and touched her. She dragged her eyes away
from him with an effort to look at her father. 'I was
hoping you'd take me out to lunch.'

'Sorry,' he said ruefully, 'I've another appointment in half an hour.'

'We've just about finished,' Brad put in as her face clouded, 'and I still have to eat. Supposing I do the honours instead?'

It was more than she had anticipated—more than she could have hoped for. Head on one side, she said lightly, 'As I hate eating alone, I'll take you up on that.'

'Fine.' Her father's attention was already distracted. 'We'll celebrate tonight—oh, lord, no, it will have to be tomorrow night. I'm seeing a client.'

'The penalties of success,' Brad sympathised. His eyes were on Kerry. 'Anywhere in particular you'd like to go?'

She said the first name that came to mind. 'Simpson's?'

'Too stuffy. How about Tiddy Dols?'

Green eyes took on a fresh sparkle. 'Obviously a man of decision!'

He laughed. 'It goes with the job.'

They made small talk during the drive across town. Seated in the restaurant, with drinks in front of them and their order taken, Brad lifted his glass to her. 'Once again—congratulations!' The toast drunk, he added casually, 'So what are your plans from here on?'

There was no harm in telling him, Kerry decided, even though she would have preferred her father to be the first to hear it.

'University to start with,' she said. 'I've applied for a degree course.'

'Good for you. In what?'

'Civil engineering. I aim to be as good as Dad is one day.'

'Some ambition.' His tone was easy. 'Does he know?'

'Not yet. I wanted to be sure I'd made the grades before I told him.' She was watching his face, her brightness damped a little. 'You don't seem to think much of the idea.'

He shrugged. 'I've nothing against women in engineering, providing they stick to what they can handle. The kind of jobs your father takes on might be a bit outside your scope, that's all.'

'The kind of job *you* do might be outside my scope,' she rejoined. 'You don't need shoulders like an ox to design a bridge!'

His grin lent an almost boyish quality to the lean features for a moment. 'Is that a fact?'

She had to smile back. 'It's an observation. Anyway, time will tell.'

'That's for sure.' The grey eyes were openly appraising. 'Wonderful to be eighteen with all the choices still in front of you.'

'You talk as if your own were limited,' she scoffed. 'How old *are* you, anyway?'

He lifted a quizzical eyebrow. 'Take a guess.'

'Twenty-eight,' she hazarded.

'I'm thirty. Nearly old enough to be your father.'

'You'd have had to be a very advanced twelve-year-old.' Her tone was impatient. 'Stop playing the heavy with me, Brad. I'm mature enough to see through you.'

He said very softly, 'With what conclusions?'

Kerry made herself hold his gaze. 'I think you're as attracted to me as I am to you.'

The laugh held genuine amusement. 'You don't believe in holding back, do you?'

'Why bother? Life's too short to waste time in subterfuge.'

'Not at eighteen.'

'You're obsessed with age!'

'Or lack of it.' He shook his head at her. 'Save it for some lucky youth you're still to meet.'

'I wasn't offering you my body,' she came back smartly. 'Just telling you how I feel. Boys my own age are so... unimpressive.'

'Or plain intimidated.'

She widened her eyes at him with deliberation, enjoying the exchange. 'Do I intimidate you?'

'Totally.' He was smiling, but there was something in his eyes that made her heart quicken its beat. 'Your course instructors just don't know what's coming to them!'

'Term doesn't start for another month,' she said meaningfully. 'When do you have to go?'

'Couple of weeks.'

'Do you have any plans for them?'

The laugh came again. 'If I did, I've a fancy they're going to go by the board!'

For Kerry, everything went by the board during those next tumultuous days—including telling her father of her future plans. Questioned, she replied evasively, her thoughts centred on the man who had already come to mean so much to her. Love took precedence over ambition when it arrived with such devastating force.

Dining with him, dancing with him, just being with him was everything she had ever dreamed about. Had he made the move, she would have given herself to him without compunction before the week was out. He wanted her, she knew that, but his lovemaking was always restrained.

'I won't break,' she told him that final night. 'I'm a woman, Brad, not a child!'

'You're a witch,' he murmured. 'A green-eyed, devastating little witch. What the hell am I going to do with you?'

They were in the car he had hired, saying goodnight outside her home. 'You could always marry me,' she whispered against his mouth, and felt him go so very still.

'And what do you think your father would have to say to that?' he asked after a moment or two.

'He doesn't even know I've been seeing you,' she confessed, 'but he'd accept it if it was what I wanted.'

'And your career?'

'I'd have a different one, that's all.' At that moment she meant every word. 'I could travel with you. Live locally. I always wanted to see the world.'

'You don't know what you're talking about.' His tone had roughened. 'You're going to university.'

'I don't care about university. I care about you!' She kissed him feverishly, pressing herself to him. 'Make love to me, Brad!'

He seized her arms, pulling them from around his neck and setting her back into her seat. His face was shadowed, but nothing could disguise the set of his jaw.

'Listen to me,' he said gruffly, 'I made one bad mistake letting you get to me at all—I don't intend making another. The last thing I need is a wife trailing around after me. Do I make myself clear?'

It was like having her heart torn out by brute force. She could only sit there looking at him, searching the hard features for some sign of the man she had believed him to be.

'I said, do I make myself clear?' he repeated in the same unemotional tone, galvanising her into jerky movement as she fumbled for the door lever.

'Perfectly,' she choked, and thought her throat would rip with the pain of it. 'You're an out-and-out louse, Brad!'

There was a certain wryness in the tilt of his lip. 'Through and through, sweetheart!'

She got out of the car, closing the door again with a control she had to fight to retain. She could see him through the window, his hand already reaching for the ignition as if he couldn't wait to be rid of her. Then the car was moving away, leaving her standing there on the pavement with love turned to a hatred so intense it filled every fibre of her being.

It was a week before she saw him again. A week during which she immersed herself in preparations for the university course she had been so ready to abandon. Never again, she vowed, was she going to let a man come between her and her aims. From now on, personal relationships took a definite second place. Love was a mug's game, anyway.

She was shopping in Oxford Street when she saw Brad handing a dark-haired young woman, little older than she was herself, into a waiting taxi. On impulse, she hailed a second cab and told the driver to follow, gaining compliance without question from a man obviously accustomed to odd requests.

He was quite prepared to make a slow pass of the other vehicle when it finally stopped to deposit its passengers outside one of the smart boutiques on Kensington High Street, giving her the opportunity to see Brad bend and kiss the girl on the lips before she went into the shop, then get back into the waiting taxi.

'Let me out here, please,' Kerry told her driver round the next corner.

He did so, accepting the generous tip with an air of indifference. Still not really sure of her intentions, Kerry walked back to the boutique and pretended to look in the window while she mulled things over. If Brad was playing another vulnerable girl along, then it was time something was done. It might be just a game to him, but she didn't want anyone else to get hurt the way she had been hurt. Revenge, she told herself self-righteously, was only a small part of it.

There were several young women assistants, she saw, when she got inside; none of them was the one she was looking for. Only after browsing for some minutes did she finally spot the dark head over some racks at the rear of the premises.

There was no one else near when she reached her. 'I'd like a word with you,' she said quickly before she could change her mind.

An automatic smile lighting her strikingly attractive features, the girl looked at her enquiringly. 'Yes, madam?'

'You were with Brad Halston a few minutes ago.'

Fine brows drew together. 'Well, yes.'

'Then I think I should warn you about him.'

The puzzlement grew. 'Warn me?'

Kerry's hesitation was brief enough to be almost non-existent. 'He's out for a good time, that's all—regardless of who gets hurt in the process. I should know. I got dumped only last week. I'd hate for the same thing to happen to you.'

The girl's eyes darkened. 'Brad wouldn't act that way!'

'If you believe that you obviously don't know him very well.' The rancour boiling up inside swamped any remaining scruples. 'What he wants he takes—with or without consent!'

There was shocked comprehension in the other's expression. 'You're saying he...used force on you?'

A red light went on at the back of Kerry's mind, but she ignored it. 'Call it what you like. Just take heed of it, that's all!'

It wasn't until she was outside again that the full realisation of what she had said struck her. For a brief moment she hovered on the verge of going back and retracting the insinuation, but pride was stronger than shame. She had already made a fool of herself once; she couldn't face that girl in there again.

If she passed on the story to Brad instead of simply giving him his marching orders, then there was every possibility that he was going to come looking for an explanation—something else that hadn't occurred to her. Either way, she thought unhappily, it was time she stepped back and took a good long look at herself...

That had probably been the turning-point in her progress towards adulthood, Kerry reflected. She might have made it even faster if Brad had indeed come looking for her, but he hadn't. Now, four years later, he appeared to regard the whole episode with indifference.

'You're wasting your time giving me the evil eye,' he said without turning his head. 'I'm immune.'

'With a skin as thick as yours, you'd have to be,' she retorted. 'No one else matters providing you come out on top!'

His laugh was humourless. 'So far as you're concerned, I consider myself more sinned against than sinning. I was pretty well tempted to put some substance to that claim of yours before I left. Given the opportunity, I might just renew the urge.'

'If that's a threat,' she said scathingly, 'I'm not impressed. I'm here with my father's full backing. You can't deny me access to his own staff quarters.'

'Try me,' he invited. 'I've got men up there who haven't seen anything like you in months. We're coming up to completion. The last thing needed now is a distraction.'

'You're willing to admit I could actually distract you?' she queried with irony, and saw his lip tilt.

'I was talking about the men. Work would stop every time you came into view.'

She said coolly, 'I think you're overestimating the reaction.'

'I doubt it.'

'All right, so they'd soon get used to my being there.'

'They're not going to get the chance. How many times do I have to say it? What you do when we get to Las Meridas is your own concern, but you're *not* coming up to the site! Understood?'

It was hopeless arguing with him. Kerry turned away without answering to look down through the port at the mountains spreading to south and west in a never-ending succession of ridges. There were villages down there, she had read, which could be reached only by *burro*. Seeing the ruggedness of the terrain, she could well believe it. Only occasionally could she pick out the thin thread of a road.

Las Meridas was accessible, of course. Three hours by road from Ciudad Victoria, the guidebooks said. With electricity provided by the turbines installed as part of the scheme, the whole area would open up.

'How long were you in Mexico City?' she asked, determined not to indulge in any lengthy silences.

'Two days,' he said. 'A weekend meeting with the powers-that-be.'

'Problems?'

He shook his head. 'As a matter of fact, we're ahead of schedule.'

'As consultant engineer, Dad still has to certify completion, though.'

'Try telling me something I don't know,' he came back derisively.

Her tone was equally cutting. 'You mean there might *be* something? You haven't changed, Brad!'

'You never really knew me,' he said.

'As much as I needed to know!' She took a grip on herself, aware of the futility in going over old ground. 'How long before we land?'

He accepted the change of subject without demur. 'Another couple of hours. You'll need somewhere to stay tonight.'

'I imagine there are hotels?'

'None I'd care to recommend.' There was a pause. When he spoke again it was with a certain resignation. 'You'd better stay at the same place I'll be staying.'

She looked at him in surprise. 'You won't be going straight up to the dam?'

'No point. The road up is risky enough in daylight, especially at this time of the year. I'll be leaving first thing in the morning.'

And she wouldn't be far behind him, Kerry vowed. Project manager or not, he couldn't forcibly eject her from the site!

CHAPTER TWO

SEEN from the air, Las Meridas looked a fairly sizeable township nestled in a broad valley between two ranges. The sun was close to the western mountain rim when they landed, softening the contours of the surrounding landscape and casting purple shadows across the single strip of concrete.

With no checked baggage to bother about himself, Brad waited with ill-concealed impatience for Kerry's to be brought through to the shack which served as the terminal building.

'Just the one?' he queried with irony, when she indicated the brown leather holdall.

'I came with the intention of learning,' she retorted, 'not putting on a fashion parade! Trousers, shirts and a couple of pairs of overalls about sums it up. Hardly likely to constitute a distraction.'

'Depends what's in them,' he returned. 'You could wear sackcloth and ashes, and it would still be no go.'

'You'll have to answer to my father for this,' she warned wrathfully.

He shrugged. 'OK by me.'

Outside, he secured the services of a battered taxi-cab, addressing the driver in Spanish. It was dark enough by now to cloak the immediate scenery, although the mountains were still visible against the skyline. A clutch of generator-fed lights outlined the more important buildings in the main plaza. Of the people moving around, many wore the traditional dress of the Indian, with the men sporting flattish straw hats bedecked with ribbons. There seemed to be a *cantina* on every other corner.

Their destination lay on the outskirts of the town up a narrow street angling towards the mountains. Brad paid off the taxi, and hoisted Kerry's bag along with his own, despite her protests, to pass through a stone archway into a tiny enclosed courtyard. At the top of a short flight of steps, he indicated she should knock on the door.

What Kerry had been expecting by way of a host or hostess, she wasn't entirely sure, but a blonde-haired, stunningly attractive American wasn't it. The latter's eyes failed to find her immediately. Her attention was all for the man on whom the light fell.

'Hi!' she exclaimed. 'I was beginning to think you'd missed the flight.'

'They were a long time getting the bags off.' His tone was easy—suggesting long acquaintance. 'I've brought you a visitor for the night. She'll be going back to Monterrey on tomorrow's flight. Can do?'

A way of putting it that left little option, Kerry thought drily, moving forwards as the other shifted her gaze. 'Sorry to drop on you like this,' she said. 'I wasn't given much choice.'

To the woman's credit, the smile turned on looked entirely genuine. 'No hassle. Come on in.'

Downstairs, the house consisted of one large living area, simply though comfortably furnished. The floor was bare wood, save for the scattering of rugs. Colourful Indian blankets draped the deep sofa and chairs.

'Make yourself at home,' the American woman invited. 'Supper will be ready in two shakes.'

'This is Kerry Wallace,' supplied Brad. 'Rina Nixon.'

The deep blue eyes held a friendly enough light. 'A bit of a flying trip, isn't it?'

'It wasn't intended to be,' Kerry acknowledged. 'I'm supposed to join the consultant team up at the dam site.'

'Oh?' Rina looked puzzled. 'So what's the problem?'

'I am,' Brad cut in. 'It's no place for a woman.'

Her glance went from him to Kerry and back again, gaining some indefinable expression in the process. 'Surely that depends on her reasons for being there?'

'Don't *you* start,' he growled. 'I'm not entering into any debate on sexual equality. Not where this job's concerned, at any rate. All she needs is a bed for the night.'

'Sure.' There was a kind of wry humour in the glance she sent Kerry's way this time. 'I'll take you up to the room. You might like to freshen up.'

Kerry picked up her bag and accompanied Rina up the narrow staircase without looking in Brad's direction, afraid of what she might say if she caught that sardonic smile on his lips. He could make any declaration he liked; it didn't mean she had to accept it. Once she reached the site, she would have the resident engineer himself to back her up. He certainly had as much authority as anyone on the construction team.

The room to which Rina showed her had a bed and a chair and little else, but it looked spotlessly clean.

'Sorry for the lack of refinements,' the other proffered at her back. 'I rented the place as it came.'

'It's fine,' Kerry assured her. 'I'm hardly going to be here long enough to need anything more.' She added curiously, 'Have you lived in Las Meridas long?'

'Three months,' came the answer. 'I originally intended only staying a couple, but it stretched.'

Because of Brad? Kerry wondered fleetingly, and felt a sharp little pang under her ribcage.

'Extended vacation?' she hazarded.

Rina smiled, showing a set of excellent teeth. 'I came here to paint. The area offers a limitless scope to the landscape artist. Plus I needed to get away for a spell. A man,' she tagged on levelly, 'in case you're wondering. The source of most female ills!'

'You seem so self-sufficient,' Kerry murmured.

The shrug was light. 'I'm learning to be.' There was a pause, a change of expression. 'What's the real story with you and Brad?'

Kerry eyed her with what she hoped was suitably surprised enquiry. 'I'm sorry?'

'There has to be more to it than simple male chauvinism. I take it you are fully qualified?'

It was Kerry's turn to shrug. 'On paper, yes. So far as converting theory into practice goes, I'm still a babe in arms.'

'Which you stand to remain unless you can get the experience on site.'

'In a nutshell.' Kerry warmed to the seemingly genuine understanding. 'I knew Brad some years ago when I was just a teenager. I think he still sees me the same way.'

'Short-sighted of him. You don't come across as immature.'

'Thanks. He's scared I might cause trouble among the workforce.'

'Only if you started playing them off against one another, and I doubt if you're the type.'

Kerry's answering smile was wry. 'Try convincing Brad of that!'

'Take more than me.' Rina let the subject drop. 'There's a bathroom of sorts next door. I pumped a tankful of water up earlier, so you should be OK. It's well water, by the way, so it can be drunk without puri-

fying first. Cold for now, I'm afraid. I have to boil all
I need on the kitchen stove.'

'I can manage,' Kerry assured her.

Left alone, she got up again to lift her bag on to the
bed for want of anywhere else to put it. At this height
above sea level the nights were cool. A pair of trousers
and a light cotton sweater would provide adequate protection indoors. Outside, she would probably need a
jacket, too.

Tomorrow was going to be the real test. Once Brad
was out of the way she had to find transport of her own.
The site was some twenty kilometres from the town itself,
which didn't sound too bad. Despite what Brad had said,
there had to be a fairly well-defined road in order for
them to have got all the machinery up there in the first
place, so it shouldn't take longer than a couple of hours
at the most. Self-drive hire might be the best idea.
Someone could always follow her down to return the
vehicle.

Brad's autocratic refusal to allow her access to the site
made her blood boil every time she thought about it.
His stated reason was just an excuse. He was taking the
opportunity to pay her back for putting a spoke in his
wheel four years ago.

Always providing the girl in question had reacted the
way Kerry had wanted her to react, that was. Perhaps
he had been able to persuade her that the insinuation
wasn't true. He had left England only a few days later,
so the affair could scarcely have been a lengthy one,
whatever the outcome.

Beside the point, anyway, she reflected. Her concern
was with the present. Nothing and no one was going to
deflect her from her aim—if she had to fight tooth and
nail to maintain it!

The bathroom was basic in the extreme but she managed well enough. She would be roughing it for the next few weeks, so this was good practice. Apart from a smear of moisturiser, she did without make-up. Her hair she fastened back into her nape with a slide, viewing the finished result with a certain grim satisfaction. Hardly the *femme fatale*. Most men wouldn't even give her a second glance!

An appetising aroma floated up to meet her as she descended to the living-room again. Brad lounged in one of the easy chairs, a glass in his hand. He looked, she thought, completely at home.

'Trying to tell me something?' he asked on a sardonic note. 'The schoolgirl look would be a sure-fire winner with some I could think of.'

'You should know,' Kerry returned pointedly. 'I'm not out to impress.'

'You're wasting your time if you think you might get me to change my mind,' he stated flatly. 'All you've done is underline the reasons why not. It's a man's world up there. I aim to keep it that way.'

She controlled an urge to go over and wipe that slant from his lips with a well-aimed swing. Brad Halston was no gentleman. There was every chance he might swing right back. How she could ever have found him so devastatingly attractive, she couldn't begin to imagine. The folly of youth, she reflected without humour. That masculine arrogance of his might have impressed her at eighteen; all it did now was irritate.

Rina came through from what appeared to be the kitchen, carrying a steaming dish which she deposited on the plain deal table. 'I hope you like chillies,' she said.

'I like most foods,' Kerry assured her. She took the chair indicated, savouring the smell of garlic and tomatoes issuing forth from the big stewpot. 'That looks delicious!'

'One of my favourites,' Brad announced, joining them at the table. 'They're hotter than the European version, so be careful. If you start at the small end you'll have time to acclimatise before you get to the stem.'

'I hardly need a blueprint,' she returned shortly, and saw the mobile left eyebrow flick upwards.

'Suit yourself.'

It had been a childish retort, and she knew it, but it was too late now to retract. She directed a smile in Rina's direction instead as the latter spooned a couple of the smallish peppers on to her plate along with a generous helping of the sauce in which they had been stewed. 'They're stuffed, aren't they?'

'With cheese,' agreed the other. 'Then dipped in egg batter and fried before going into the sauce. Not a dish for the diet-conscious—though you hardly need to worry about *your* weight.'

That made two of them, Kerry thought drily. Touching thirty though she might be, the American woman's figure was still as taut and supple as her own. She wore little make-up either, her blonde hair cut to frame her high-cheekboned face. The kind of looks that would wear well; certainly the kind to attract a man of Brad's ilk. Not that it was any concern of hers whether or not the two of them were involved.

The chillies, as Brad had warned her, were hotter than any she had tasted before. It was all she could do to keep chewing on that first mouthful. Eyes watering, she took more care with the next. Neither Rina nor he appeared to be having any trouble. They must, she thought sourly, have asbestos-lined throats!

'Don't feel you have to finish it,' Rina advised on a casual note. 'They're an acquired taste. I made *buñuelos* for dessert. You'll find those filling enough.'

'Another of your favourites?' Kerry asked Brad sweetly. 'Aren't you the lucky guy!'

There was a distinct spark in the grey eyes, but his tone was easy enough. 'The best restaurant in town!'

Rina laughed. 'The cheapest, I'll grant you.'

The glance he rested on her held an expression Kerry found disturbing. 'You'll receive your just reward in heaven.'

'I'd as soon not take a chance on finishing up there,' she came back lightly. 'More wine, Kerry?'

Kerry had drained her glass in a vain attempt to quench the burning in her mouth. She nodded, ignoring the light-headedness already overtaking her. Getting drunk seemed a good idea right now, although she couldn't fully have explained why.

Brad watched her attack the second glass without comment. His very size made the room seem smaller, more confining. The lamplight flickered across strong features, and her stomach muscles tensed in a way she recognised only too well. She was suddenly sorry she had ever made this trip, suddenly desperate to be back home in England again. Nothing was turning out the way she had anticipated.

The evening seemed to dissolve into a series of impressions after that. She was vaguely aware at one point of moving from the table to the sofa; of conversation washing over her as she sank deeper and deeper into the trough of despondency.

Her eyelids were heavy. She closed them for a moment or two, feeling herself lift and float through the air. When she opened her eyes again Brad's face swam into view, close enough to feel his breath on her cheek and see the shadow that would be the morning's beard along his jawline.

'Get some sleep,' he said, depositing her on the bed and standing back. 'You've a ten-thirty flight to make.'

Her voice seemed to be coming from a long distance away. 'I hate your guts!'

His lips twisted. 'Not as much as you might. Goodbye, Kerry. I'll be gone before you surface.'

She awoke to sunlight, lying still for a moment wondering where on earth she was until memory supplied the answer in depressing detail.

Apart from a certain dryness, she at least had no after-effects from the wine she had drunk last night, she realised thankfully when she sat up. She was stripped down to her undies, yet she had no recollection of getting undressed.

Brad's face was the last thing she remembered seeing. He wouldn't have—would he?

Far more likely that Rina had helped her out of her clothing, she reassured herself. Hardly an ideal way to thank her for her hospitality. She had never known wine go to her head as quickly.

A light tap on the door heralded the entry of her hostess.

'Oh, good, you're awake!' she exclaimed. 'I put some hot water in the bathroom for you. You have a couple of hours to make that flight.'

'Brad already left?' Kerry asked diffidently.

'Soon as it was light. What do you usually eat for breakfast?'

'Coffee and toast will be fine, if they're available.'
She made a jerky movement as the other woman began
to turn away. 'Rina.'

The blonde head turned. 'Yes?'

'I just wanted to say sorry for passing out on you last
night, that's all. I don't normally act that way.'

The answering smile was encouraging. 'More travel
weariness than anything. Don't worry about it.'

'Brad made the same journey,' Kerry pointed out,
intent on self-flagellation.

'So he's out of a different mould.' One hand came up
in a dismissive gesture. 'Forget it. See you downstairs
when you're ready.'

The hot water was more than welcome. Washed and
dried, she put on the same trousers and a clean shirt
from her case, then brushed her hair into its usual heavy
rope. There seemed little point in trying to tone down
her looks before she even reached the site. Time enough
for that after she settled *how* she was going to get there.

She found Rina seated at a rickety iron table out on
a small rear patio when she eventually went down. From
here there was an excellent view of the town, its white-
walled buildings sparkling in the morning sunlight.

The mountains formed a spectacular backcloth: a
barrier against the outside world only penetrated to any
real extent during the last fifty years or so. The dis-
covery of vast new silver deposits in the locality had put
Las Meridas squarely on the map. A year from now,
with the dam supplying both water and electricity, the
town would be a thriving metropolis.

'Help yourself,' Rina invited, pushing the earth-
enware coffee-pot towards her as she took a seat. 'I'll
get the toast.'

'I can make it myself,' Kerry offered quickly. 'You don't have to wait on me hand and foot.'

'It won't take a minute.' Rina was already at the door. 'Just sit tight.'

It took more like five. When she returned she was carrying a loaded plate.

'Afraid the place doesn't run to a rack,' she said. 'Doesn't run to much at all in the way of equipment. The cooking's done on a charcoal grill—including the toast, so don't be too surprised by the flavour.'

'It'll be fine,' Kerry assured her, reaching for a slice. 'I'm not all that hungry, anyway.'

'You're not likely to get anything else until you get to Monterrey.'

Kerry took a bite of the toast, chewed and swallowed before dropping her bombshell. 'I'm not going to Monterrey.'

The American woman studied her for a long moment, her expression hard to read. 'What's the alternative?'

'I'll make my own way up to the site.'

'Brad will still be there.'

'So will the resident engineer. He'll soon put him right.'

'He will?' The tone was sceptical. 'I was under the impression the resident engineer was there in a supervisory capacity only.'

'In a sense,' Kerry agreed. 'It still doesn't alter the fact that Brad was overstepping his authority. My father is the consultant. Surely that gives him the right to choose his own site staff?'

'Put that way, I guess it does.' She gave a smiling shrug. 'Best of luck, whatever.'

Kerry allowed a moment or two to pass before asking, 'Any idea where I might hire myself a car?'

'You'll need a four-wheel drive to get where you're going,' Rina answered. 'We had a storm yesterday. It could have caused problems on the road up. You could try Miguel's, I guess. He runs the only gas station in town at present. He might just have something suitable.'

'Sounds good enough.' Kerry refused to allow herself to be put off. 'How do I find him?'

'Straight down the street, turn right for a couple of blocks and you'll see the sign.'

That settled, it was time to change the subject, Kerry judged. 'Is the painting just a hobby?' she asked on a casual note.

Blue eyes registered a certain wry humour. 'I sell one from time to time.'

'But you don't keep any on display?'

'I use the loft as a studio. What I've done so far is up there.'

Kerry waited expectantly, but the invitation to view apparently wasn't going to be forthcoming. 'How did you and Brad meet up?' she asked at length.

'Market day a couple of weeks after I got here. I was about to be well and truly fleeced until he stepped in. I'm useless at bartering. They see me coming a mile off!'

'Me too,' Kerry confessed. 'I can never convince myself that it's actually an expected thing—especially when the vendor puts on that "you're taking the bread from my children's mouths" expression.' She paused before tagging on, 'I imagine Brad is very good at it, though.'

'If you mean because you consider him a hard case,' came the level response, 'then you're hardly being fair. He's a fine man. One I'd trust with my life if necessary. OK, so he takes the upper hand at times. Considering his job, it must be difficult for him to be any other way.

Cut off from home so long, the men tend to get pretty restless.'

'Then you think he's right about my going up there?'

'Oh, I wouldn't go so far as to say he's *never* wrong. As I said before, you have to get your experience somewhere. Trouble is, I can see both sides.'

Pity she couldn't teach Brad to do the same, Kerry thought acidly. She drained her coffee-cup and put it down, pushing back her chair. 'I'd better go and see about that transport. Thanks again for everything, Rina.'

The other's smile made light of the moment. 'You're more than welcome. Drop in next time you're down. The whole town is under siege every weekend.'

And where did Brad spend his weekends? Kerry wondered, going to fetch her things downstairs. There was something more than casual friendship between the two of them, for certain. How much more remained an open question. With only two bedrooms in the house, it was likely they had shared the other last night.

Her mind shied away from the images suggested by that thought.

It was just gone ten when she left the house. Rina had offered to take her down to the *automotriz*, but she thought it best if the American woman took no further hand in her actions. The last thing she wanted, she told herself with emphasis, was to cause any bad blood between her and Brad.

The sun was hot, her bag weightier than it had felt yesterday. Far more than twenty-four hours seemed to have passed since she had left Mexico City. What would the next twenty-four bring?

Miguel's proved easy enough to find by virtue of the fuel pump stuck in the middle of the narrow forecourt. Miguel himself was a man of indeterminate years and considerable girth, whose indolent manner belied the sharpness of his dark eyes. As he spoke no English, it took her a little time to get her request across to him, only to receive a sorrowful shake of his head when she finally succeeded.

No four-wheel drive, he declared. He took her round to the rear of the premises to show her what was available. Studying the two small battered saloons, she knew a twinge of doubt. From what Rina had said, the road up to the dam site might well be impassable at present to normal front-wheel drive.

On the other hand, what choice did she have? If the worst came to the worst, she would simply have to turn back and wait for a more favourable time.

Settling the hire fee took even more time. In the end, she simply laid notes on the table in what passed for an office until the man nodded enough. No way to do business, she conceded wryly, but short of going back up the hill to appeal for Rina's help, there was no other method available. At least the price included a full tank and, from what she could glean, gave her a week before return.

After all that, ascertaining the route she needed to take out of town proved surprisingly easy. One mention of the dam and Miguel obligingly drew her a rough map. His curiosity as to her business there was obvious, but the lack of verbal communication would have ruled out any explanations even if she had been prepared to supply them.

The car she had chosen started after some coaxing. The engine sounded rough, the bodywork even noisier. A case of a wing and a prayer, Kerry thought with determined humour. All she had to do was keep it going over the outward journey. If it broke down after that, it would be up to Miguel himself to get it back.

He was still standing gazing after her when she turned the corner at the end of the street. There were plenty of people around. Market day, she realised on reaching the central plaza. A colourful spectacle well worth a photograph, had she brought a camera with her. Essentials only had been the general rule.

Two hours later she was beginning to regret that lack of a camera even more. The scenery was magnificent, the surrounding peaks jutting from the tree line like jagged teeth to stand out in relief against a sky so blue it hurt the eyes. So far the dirt road had been reasonably clear, although she had only managed about fourteen kilometres due to the steepness of the gradients and the lack of pulling power in the car engine. At this rate, she reckoned, it was going to take her at least another hour to make the site. She had brought neither food nor drink with her, which perhaps had been a little short-sighted, but going without lunch was no real hardship. No doubt she'd be able to get something to eat when she reached her destination.

She put another kilometre on the clock before she ran into the first spot of trouble. A series of tiny streams coming down the mountainside had made a quagmire of the road surface. Overflow from yesterday's storm, she surmised, engaging first gear to pick her way gingerly through the muddy pot-holes.

Within a few hundred yards she was in trouble again, this time from scattered rocks. Brad had obviously made it through, she reflected. Where he could go, so could she!

How wrong she was on that score was brought home to her barely seconds later when one rock she hadn't even seen took out the sump. Heart in her brogue-type shoes, she cut the engine and got out of the car to see the sunlight picking out colour in the stream of sludgy oil running from beneath the vehicle. That was that, wasn't it? She could go no further.

More to the point, the realisation followed, she had no way of letting anyone know what had happened. Until someone or something happened along she was totally stuck.

Site deliveries had to be made from time to time even at this late stage, she reassured herself. Food alone must be a major requirement; not all of it could be stored on any long-term basis. All she had to do was sit tight and wait.

Thinking was one thing, doing quite another. Even the scenery began to pall a little after gazing at it for an hour or more. Birdsong was the only sound to break the stillness. Small green parakeets seemed to abound in the area.

The first indication of rescue came from up ahead. Not a car, Kerry judged, getting out of her own vehicle again to listen to the slowly approaching engine sound. More like a tractor—or a bulldozer.

Coming down to clear the road, of course! Brad must have reported the fall on his arrival earlier. As he was hardly likely to be driving the machine himself, she could no doubt beg a lift the rest of the way.

The car she could do little about. In truth, it was hardly worth the cost of repair, although Miguel would more than likely disagree with that assessment. Eventually it would have to be towed back to the town, but she would cross that bridge when she came to it. At present, her sole concern was reaching her destination.

Appearing round the bend of the road like one of the more minor prehistoric monsters, the bulldozer came to a sudden stop as the driver saw her standing there. He was about Brad's age, or maybe a bit younger, Kerry judged. From the expression on his face, lone women were a rarity in the area. At least he was Anglo. Trying to explain her presence to one of the locals might have proved difficult.

'Bit off the beaten track, aren't you?' he shouted above the engine noise. 'There's nothing up here apart from the dam.'

'That's where I'm headed,' she shouted back. 'Can you turn that thing off for a minute?'

He did so, then got down from the cabin, tipping his hard hat back over dusty brown hair as he studied her.

'You say you're on your way to the dam?'

'That's right.' She was aware of a certain discomfiture under the frank appraisal. Stripped at a glance, was one way of putting it. She forced herself to disregard the feeling. This man's help was needed. Stepping on her high horse wasn't going to help matters. 'I imagine you're here to clear the road?'

'Too late, by the look of it,' he returned, casting a glance in the direction of the car. 'Yours?'

'Hired,' she said. 'From Las Meridas.'

'Miguel, eh? Means it was on its last legs, anyway. No loss if I shove it over the side.'

'You can't do that!' she protested.

'Can't leave it stuck in the middle of the road, either. There's a delivery expected this afternoon.' He sounded unconcerned. 'Miguel isn't going to fetch it down, you can bet. If I know him, he'll have made enough on the hiring to cover his losses.'

Recalling what she had paid, Kerry could see his point. All the same, she couldn't countenance just tipping the vehicle. 'What about the environment?' she asked weakly.

He shrugged. 'Be hidden in the trees down there till it rusts away.' There was curiosity in his eyes. 'Looking for somebody in particular?'

'I'm joining the consultant staff,' she explained for what seemed like the umpteenth time. 'Is there going to be room for me in the cabin?'

His grin was slow and not a little suggestive. 'You bet! Just give me five minutes.'

She went to get her bag from the car as he climbed back into the cab again. Standing back under the lee of the mountainside, she watched him lower the blade and start clearing the rockfall from the road by the simple process of pushing the rubble over the edge where the ground fell away down to the line of trees.

Heavy though the car was, it was no match against the steady advance, vanishing the same way with a crashing, rending sound which echoed throughout the valley.

With the machine turned back in its tracks, she lost no time in getting aboard. The cabin was cramped with two of them in. The only way she could sit down was to squeeze in behind the driver's seat and perch on her suitcase.

'The name's Pete Lomas, by the way,' he said.

'Kerry Wallace,' she supplied.

'First time we had a female on site.' He sounded anything but despondent over the prospect.

'There's a first time for everything,' she said with what lightness she could muster, and heard him laugh.

'I'm always ready to try a new experience!'

For Kerry the journey was a pain in more ways than one. Long before they reached the site, she was wishing herself anywhere but in this cab with this man. It wasn't so much what he said but the way he said it: every word loaded with innuendo. Turning a seemingly deaf ear served little apparent purpose, but helped her keep her temper under control. If this was an example of what she might expect from the rest of the crew, then the sooner she accustomed herself to it, the better. They were only words, after all.

She had her first sight of the dam from the head of the valley. Sited on top of an escarpment, the graceful arch spanned the gap between two buttresses of rock guarding the upper gorge. The road they were following led to the bottom of the escarpment where men and machinery were at work, then wound in a series of zigzags up the hillside to the dam crest.

The generator house was almost finished, she saw as they drew nearer. In three months the valley beyond would be under water, the turbines supplying the power that would bring Las Meridas to full and profitable life. It was an exciting thought.

They passed the living quarters halfway down the valley. A well-ordered lay-out from the look of it, with prefabricated buildings providing substantial accommodation. Closer to the work site itself, another couple of low, square buildings suggested offices—a guess confirmed when Pete Lomas brought the bulldozer to a halt in front of the nearest one.

'You'll find the resident engineer in there,' he said. 'First door you come to. See you later, maybe?'

Not if she saw him first! Kerry thought. 'Thanks for the lift,' she said, and hoisted her bag to move purposefully across the few feet of flattened earth.

A murmur of voices came from within the room indicated. It seemed politic to knock before going in. The voice inviting her to enter was short, as if the interruption might have come at a bad moment, but it was too late now to retreat.

Recognisable from the several times she had met him, Alan Pope was standing at the drawing-board, his back to the door as he continued talking to the man facing him. Just like that very first time, came the fleeting thought as the words of greeting faded on her lips.

Except that there was no friendly speculation in the look Brad was giving her this time. The grey eyes held nothing but sheer blazing anger.

CHAPTER THREE

'STILL not prepared to take no for an answer, I see,' Brad said grimly. 'How the hell did you get here, anyway?'

'I drove up,' said Kerry with surface composure. 'As far as the landslide, that is. Your 'dozer driver gave me a lift from there.'

'Did he!'

From the tone, Pete Lomas was going to find himself on the rough end of a tongue-lashing in the near future. Kerry couldn't find it in herself to be too sorry about that—although she should be grateful to him, she supposed, for bringing her this far. Not that there had been any real choice when it all boiled down. He could scarcely have left her there on the mountainside.

The other man was looking somewhat confused. He hadn't, she gathered, even been told of her arrival in Las Meridas. She smiled at him. 'Sorry about this, Alan. Dad said to give you his regards.'

Now in his mid-forties, Alan Pope had been with the firm for years. His thin features relaxed for a moment. 'He should have let me know you were actually on your way,' he said. His glance shifted questioningly to the man at his side. 'What was all that about?'

'Mr Halston here tried to deny me access to the site,' Kerry put in before he could answer.

'I'm still denying it.' His tone was curt. 'I gather you already knew she was coming?'

'Well, yes.'

'It didn't occur to you to let me in on the news?'

'I don't suppose it occurred to him that it was essential *for* you to know,' she flashed. 'Anyway, I'm here now, and I'm staying!'

The grey eyes had chips of granite in them. 'Want to take a bet on it?'

'Exactly what's going on?' Alan Pope's brows were drawn together. 'Kerry's here on her father's say-so. Of course she's staying!'

Brad turned the same hard regard on him. 'One or two things all of you seem to have overlooked—like accommodation, for instance.'

'All arranged. We did a shuffle around and freed one of the single rooms. As to the rest, we'll just have to work out a rota.' To Kerry he added, 'If that road weren't so risky I'd have suggested you stay down in the town and travel up here on a daily basis, but, as you found out for yourself, rockfalls are a regular occurrence.'

'What happened to your transport?' Brad demanded, momentarily sidetracked.

'Your driver pushed it over the side,' she said. 'He seemed to think it was past redemption.'

'If you hired it from Miguel, he was more than likely right. Trying to drive up here in one of his death-traps was sheer lunacy.'

'I didn't,' she reminded him, 'have much choice. Anyway, I was doing fine until I hit the rockfall. Death-trap or not, I don't imagine he's going to be overjoyed when he finds out what happened to his vehicle.'

'Miguel's no problem,' he retorted hardily. 'You are. What kind of effect do you think one girl's going to have on forty men?'

'It will be a twenty-four-hour novelty,' she said with deliberation. 'You're making too much of the whole thing!'

'Kerry is my responsibility.' Alan Pope's tone was deceptively mild. 'I'll see the men don't bother her.'

'I'm more concerned about her bothering the men,' came the sardonic response. 'Take a good look at her. She doesn't exactly fade into the background!'

The other cast a glance, unable to hide a faint smile. 'I'll grant you that much. All the same, you can hardly penalise somebody for looks they were born with. John obviously had no qualms about sending her out here.'

'He didn't,' she agreed. 'The only reason *you* don't want me here, Brad, is because you're bigoted against women engineers!'

His shrug suggested total indifference to the accusation. 'Maybe if you were twenty years older and thirty pounds heavier it might work out. As you're unlikely to gain either overnight, it's no odds.'

Breath coming hard and heavy, she searched her mind for some retort that would put him down where he belonged, but there was nothing forthcoming.

'It may be a long time in the future,' she managed at length, 'but one day I aim to be resident engineer myself. That means gaining as much practical experience as I can, and the only way to do it is by being on site.'

'We're almost through to completion on this job,' he rejoined. 'Not much point.'

'I can still pick up a lot on administration. Next time I'll be in from the beginning.'

'Always providing I'm not involved.'

'You've no jurisdiction over the resident engineer's choice of site staff.' She appealed to the other man for confirmation. 'Isn't that right?'

The agreement came with some slight reticence. 'On the face of it.'

There was a moment when Brad seemed set to dispute the point, then he made an curt gesture. 'As you said, she's your responsibility.'

Kerry took a step away from the doorway as he moved towards it. From the look of his jawline, it seemed advisable to give him clear passage. His capitulation had been too sudden. She hardly knew what to think.

Meeting the grey eyes for a fleeting instant as he passed, she fancied she saw contempt in their depths. So what? she asked herself forcefully as the door closed behind him. His opinions meant nothing to her. The most important point was that she had won.

Alan was looking a bit ruffled. She couldn't, she thought, blame him.

'Sorry about that,' she said wryly. 'I didn't want to be the cause of any trouble.'

'I anticipated some,' he acknowledged. 'To be honest, I wasn't too keen on the idea myself. This isn't the kind of project I'd expect a woman to take an interest in.'

'It's the only kind of project I want to be involved with,' she said. 'And I'm not about to be denied it because of an accident of birth. I'll try not to get in anyone's way.'

He nodded, then made an incisive move to flick on the intercom on the desk. 'Glenn, would you come on through for a minute?' To Kerry he said, as he released the switch again, 'My assistant, Glenn Ingram. I don't think you ever met him before?'

She shook her head, hoping the newcomer wasn't yet another bastion defender. Her reception so far left a lot to be desired. Alan himself was obviously acting under a certain duress. So it was going to be up to her to prove her ability. Allowing anyone to see she was in any way affected by the lack of welcome was definitely not a good idea.

The assistant resident engineer proved to be no more than his late twenties—a stocky young man with a cheerfully attractive face beneath a shock of sandy hair. Devoid of any hint of condescension, his greeting warmed her.

'About time the girls got a look in,' he said, shaking hands. 'Any way I can be of help, you only have to ask.'

'If you've nothing special on just now, why don't you run Kerry back to the camp and show her where she'll be sleeping?' Alan suggested. 'I'd do it myself, only...' His gesture indicated the board at his back.

'Sorry if I broke up something important,' she apologised.

'We were just about through.' He was already turning away. 'Hope you don't find conditions too primitive.'

Meaning he rather hoped she would find them too primitive to put up with, Kerry surmised, reading between the lines. She caught Glenn's eye, warming afresh to the glint of humour. At least she had one ally in camp!

'Have you eaten?' he asked when they were outside the office. 'Recently, I mean.'

'Not since breakfast,' she admitted. 'I'm not all that hungry.'

'Dinner isn't till seven, so you'd better have something to be going on with. I'll hop over to the kitchen after I show you where you'll be living, and get Joe to make you a snack.'

'If it's no trouble.'

He grinned. 'Not to me. Not to Joe, either, if I know him. The only site cook I ever met who didn't hate his job. The best one I ever knew, too. So far there hasn't been one solitary grouse about the food. That's unprecedented on a job like this.'

'No one bothers making the trip down to town, then?' she asked as they left the office block.

'Only usually at the weekends. There's a good rec. room right here on site in addition to the canteen. KDC take good care of their people. So they should. Top-grade, all of them.'

'Including Brad Halston, of course.' She couldn't keep the brittleness from her voice.

Glenn looked at her oddly. 'Run across him before, have you?'

'It was a long time ago.' She had no intention of supplying any detail. 'I didn't like him then and I don't like him now. He's too much the big I am!'

'He's one of the best agents in the business,' Glenn commented. 'He gets things done. Safety-conscious, too. Not all that much of a priority in a construction man. Time is money.'

'Talking of time,' she said, seizing on the opening, 'when does work start?'

'On site, six-thirty. An hour later for the staff. You'll be able to please yourself, of course.'

She gave him a sideways glance. 'Because my name is Wallace?'

He looked a little discomfited. 'Well, you're not on regular staff, are you?'

'I'm still here to learn, and I'm not going to do that flat on my back in bed till all hours!'

'Sorry.' He sounded chastened. 'Looks like I had the wrong idea.'

'Along with everyone else, by the look of it.' She kept her tone easy. 'You might pass the word around that I don't expect any special privileges.'

'Fair enough.' His glance held an element of admiration. 'I'm going to enjoy having you here, Kerry.'

Unlike the man who had driven her up here, he put no underlying meaning in the words. Glenn Ingram was too straight for that. A brilliant engineer, too, from what she recalled her father saying of him. Which explained how he had come so far so comparatively young. He would be resident engineer himself before he was thirty. A career path to emulate. It would leave little room for marriage, though, even with a partner involved in the same profession.

Time enough to consider that aspect, she decided, shelving the problem. There was going to be too much else to think about for the next few weeks.

The nearest of the men at work were several hundred yards away and busy loading a truck. All the same, she was aware of eyes turned in her direction. The initial confrontation would come at the evening meal. Once over that hurdle, she could start to relax.

With regard to the recreation room, she would have to wait and see. A woman's presence could well prove too uncomfortably restrictive for some. She was something of a pioneer when it came to actually living on a construction camp. One step at a time was the best way of handling it.

They took a Jeep the half-mile back to the accommodation site. Standing off to one side of the others, the smaller building had individual rooms for the senior personnel of both camps.

The one she was to occupy was at the far end of the narrow corridor. Containing a collapsible bed, a flimsy wooden wardrobe and a chest of drawers, it was scarcely big enough to swing a cat in. The brightly-hued rug on the floor was the only homely touch.

'Sorry it's so utilitarian,' Glenn apologised. 'I bought the rug to brighten it up a little.'

Kerry turned back to look at him. 'Was this your room?'

He made a throwaway gesture. 'No great sacrifice.'

'It's appreciated,' she assured him. 'Where will you be sleeping?'

He grinned. 'In with the *hoi polloi*. Some jobs I've been on, there hasn't been any choice. I'll nip along and get you that snack. Coffee and sandwiches OK?'

'Fine.' She added softly, 'And thanks.'

His fair complexion revealed a sudden tinge of added colour. 'Glad to be of service.'

He was back in what seemed like a ridiculously short time, carrying a battered tin tray.

'I had him make up a jug of coffee,' he announced, setting the tray down on the chest of drawers. 'You'll need it to get round Joe's idea of sandwiches.'

Kerry could see what he meant. Oozing sliced beef, they were thick enough to be used as doorstops! If she managed even half of one she would be doing well, she thought humorously.

'How about sharing some?' she asked.

Glenn shook his head regretfully. 'I'd better be getting on back. You never know what's going to crop up.' He paused, looking slightly embarrassed. 'The showers and other amenities are going to be most difficult part. They're communal. The men knock off at six so you've plenty of time now. The morning is going to be the main problem.'

'So I might have to wait until you're all through,' she agreed lightly, liking him all the more for his lack of insouciance. 'I'll cope, don't worry.'

'I'm sure of it.' This time the admiration was total. 'You're quite a girl, Kerry Wallace!'

He was going to be good to have around, she thought with humour after he had gone. Friend and tutor wrapped up together. Ask me anything you want to know, he'd said. She intended doing just that.

Always providing she wasn't interfering with his regular duties, that was. She had to admit that Alan Pope had some cause for restraint in his attitude. With no outlined duties of her own, she could easily finish up getting in the way of others who had. Only it wasn't going to be like that. She'd make sure it wasn't.

The coffee, half a sandwich and her unpacking were disposed of in less than twenty minutes. A shower first, she decided, then she could relax for a couple of hours.

A pair of the white overalls would make the perfect garment in which to cross the compound. Stripping off to the skin, she pulled them on and zipped up, sliding her feet into a pair of trainers she had brought along for casual wear. With towel and soap-bag over her arm, she set out to find the ablution facilities Glenn had indicated as they came in.

The other room doors were all left open. For better circulation of air, she surmised. Idle curiosity prompted a swift glance in each as she passed on her way to the main door.

All the rooms were the same size, yet each looked different according to the arrangement favoured by its occupier. In the last one, the wardrobe door had also been left open, revealing a couple of photographs pinned to the inside. It was the sight of one of these that halted her in her tracks, drawing her in after a bare moment's hesitation for a closer look.

The photograph was an enlargement of a casual snap, the dark-haired and attractive young woman smiling out of it too well remembered for there to be any mistake. A slightly older version of the same girl she had accosted in the boutique all those years ago, she realised numbly.

So this was Brad's room, and he was still involved with her. For all she knew, they could even be married. She supposed she should feel glad that her efforts to dishonour him had been unsuccessful. At least it removed some of the long-felt shame of that particular episode.

There were few items of clothing hanging in the wardrobe: a couple of pairs of trousers, ditto jeans, a lightweight jacket. A checked shirt similar to the one he was wearing at present was tossed across the bed. Beside it lay a writing-pad and pen, as if laid down halfway through a letter.

She was still standing there, fighting the temptation to take a look, when the outer door opened and Brad himself loomed into view, shoulders brushing both jambs as he came to a halt in the room doorway.

'Need any help?' he asked sardonically.

Kerry scarcely knew what to say. She had no reasonable excuse for being in his room. 'I saw that as I was passing,' she got out, with a gesture in the direction of the wardrobe.

His eyes didn't leave her face. 'What?'

'You know quite well what I'm talking about,' she flashed. 'The photograph, of course!'

'You mean Careen?'

'If that's her name, yes.' She calmed herself with an effort, to add, 'You obviously found something in her you didn't find in me. Your wife now, is she?'

He shook his head. 'I'm not married.'

Deep down, there was a stirring of some emotion too closely akin to relief. It was in an attempt to quell it that she said with sarcasm, 'Just good friends, then?'

'You might say that.' His tone was level, belying the constriction about his mouth. 'She's my kid sister.'

Shock held her motionless and silent for what seemed like an age. She could only stare at him, eyes widening as the thoughts whirled round in her head. He was telling the truth: dark hair, grey-blue eyes—the resemblance now that she knew was obvious. Why had it never occurred to her before?

Because she had been intent on seeing only the worst in him at the time, came the answer. Too late now for apologies—four years too late. Pride forbade it, anyway. The only way left was to bluff it through.

'Surprise, surprise!' she said. 'Do you have a father, too?'

His expression underwent a sudden and dangerous alteration. Moving forward, he reached behind him with deliberation and closed the room door.

'I'd have leathered the hide off you once for that,' he said grimly, 'but the satisfaction would be too short-lived right now. I thought I was past feeling cut-up about what you did until I saw you on the plane yesterday. You may be four years older, but you're sure as hell no wiser!'

Not for anything, Kerry told herself, was she going to show fear of him. If she had made a mistake in the past it was unfortunate, but her own past hurt was no less for it.

'I'm sure I'm not the first to call you a bastard,' she said with intent. 'Your path is probably strewn with broken hearts!'

The laugh was short. 'If I'd followed my inclinations you'd have suffered more than a broken heart, believe me!'

Green eyes sparked contempt. 'So what stopped you?'

'Careen did.' He paused briefly, lip curling. 'She felt you must have had some cause for feeling vindictive, even if most of it wasn't true.'

'Which I did!'

'Not enough.' There was no relaxation in the hard features. 'Short of giving up what few principles I'd managed to hang on to, there'd have been a limit to what I could have done to you at eighteen, admittedly. They say everything comes to those who wait.'

Kerry could feel her whole body tauten like a bowstring. She was conscious of his size—of the power in the muscular forearms revealed by the rolled sleeves of his shirt. When she spoke her voice sounded thick. 'What's that supposed to mean?'

'Exactly what you think it means.'

Considering the smallness of the room to start with, there was very little distance she could back away from him as he moved. Two steps, and she felt the back of her knees come up hard against the metal frame of the bed.

'Cut it out, Brad,' she said huskily. 'Touch me, and you'll have Alan Pope to contend with!'

'I'm going to do a damn sight more than touch you,' he parried. 'And he can go to hell, too!'

The hands yanking her up against him were ruthless. Kerry went rigid as she came into contact with the lean, hard length of him, every sense in her at war with her emotions. His mouth was suffocating, pressuring her lips apart. There was no tenderness in him at all, yet deep down a tiny spark began to kindle.

The use went out of her legs as he pressed her down to the bed at her back. She tried to word a protest, but the sound was caught in her throat. Then he was over and above her, his weight grinding her into the mattress. The overalls were made of fairly heavy cotton, but they were no protection. She could feel every steel-muscled line of him.

His fingers wove into her hair, holding her head still under his demanding mouth. Pinned against the wall of his chest, her breasts hurt. She beat at him with clenched fists, too well aware of the treacherous heat rising inside her; of the growing desire to stop fighting him and let matters take their course. It was in sheer desperation that she closed her teeth on his lower lip.

The dark head jerked back, but he made no move to get up.

'Bitch,' he growled.

'Let go of me!' She was hard put to it to keep any hint of pleading from her voice. 'Just get away!'

His eyes were like steel gimlets, mouth narrowed and cruel. 'Not until I'm good and ready!'

Kerry grabbed the hand moving to the zip at her throat, but it was like trying to hold on to a power wrench. She felt the metal slide downwards, the relative coolness of the air on her skin, the leap of her pulses as his fingers slid inside the gap to find her breast.

'You used to like me doing this,' he said softly, bringing the blood pounding into her ears as he rubbed the ball of his thumb over her nipple. 'I got the same reaction then, too. Try saying it now.'

'Saying what?' She had to force the words between clenched teeth, her whole body quivering with barely suppressed emotion.

'Make love to me, Brad.' His voice was taunting. 'Wasn't that how it went?' He slid the hand slowly downwards, following the curve of her waist to span her hipbone. 'If this is the outfit you were planning to wear on site, you'd have asked for everything you got!'

'Stop it.' This time she couldn't help the tremor. 'No more, Brad. Please!'

He remained quite still for a long moment looking down at her. The hand on her hip felt warm and firm, each splayed finger a separate source of torment. She wanted him to take it away, yet when he did she felt deprived. She lay there, trembling in every limb, as he pushed himself abruptly upright.

'That's just for starters,' he said on a rough note. 'If you stay on there'll be more.'

She found her voice with a supreme effort, low and shaky. 'This job means a lot to me.'

'My sister's regard means a lot to me,' came the grim response. 'I'm still not sure she was completely convinced when I denied raping you.'

Kerry moved her head on the pillow in rebuttal. 'I never said that!'

'You implied it. "What he wants he takes, with or without consent"—wasn't that how you put it?'

Guilt sparked the bitter retort. 'She must have thought you capable even to have considered it possible!'

The strong mouth twisted. 'So it seems. Not that it alters anything where you're concerned.' One hand came out again to push her down again as she made to rise. 'We're not through yet. Either you agree to get off the site, or we'll carry on where we just left off. You won't enjoy it, I can promise you that. I shan't give you the chance.'

There were times, she thought, gazing up into the unrelenting face, when discretion was indeed the better part of valour. She said huskily, 'All right, you made your point. Now will you let me up?'

'With pleasure.' He stood up himself to give her space, watching with mockery in his eyes as she tugged the zip back up again. 'It's a bit late to think about getting you back down to town today. First thing in the morning, I'll run you in myself. Rina will put you up until the next flight out on Thursday.'

'Thanks.' She kept her tone carefully neutral. 'Just as a matter of interest, what made you come back to the block in the first place?'

'I didn't intend wasting any time letting you know how things stood.'

'Even though you gave Alan the impression you'd accepted the situation?'

His lips widened briefly. 'Is that what I did?' He brought up a wrist to glance at his watch. 'Time I was getting back, anyway. It needs another couple of hours before we knock off for the day.'

'And the whole job might fall apart if you're not there to supervise!'

The sarcasm left him unmoved. 'It's my head on the block if anything goes wrong. Stay here till you're feeling up to scratch again, if you like. I shan't need the place till gone six.'

He was at the door before she said his name. It was a waste of time, and she knew it, but something in her had to make the attempt.

'Do you think Careen would approve of your methods?' she asked softly as he turned his head.

Grey eyes studied her with an indecipherable expression. 'The grudge is mine,' he said, 'not hers. A side issue, in any case. I just don't want you on site.'

'And what exactly *am* I supposed to tell Alan—or Dad, either, if it comes to that?'

The shrug was indifferent. 'That's your problem. I got what I came for.'

Not yet, he hadn't, she thought grimly as he went out. Tomorrow was a whole new day!

CHAPTER FOUR

KERRY found the facilities basic but bearable. A matter of mental adjustment, she told herself firmly. One had to learn to take the rough with the smooth in this job. At least the water was warm.

The compound itself was bare earth. When the rainy season really got under way, it would probably turn to a regular sea of mud, she judged. Mud she could no doubt deal with; Brad was in a league of his own. Not that she was going to let that make any difference. She was here and she was staying, no matter what threats he came up with. If the matter was looked at rationally, there was little enough he could do. If he made any further attempts to get to her she would simply threaten to yell rape. That should take care of things.

The memory of her response to his handling, rough as it had been, she refused to contemplate. He had taken her by surprise, that was all. If there was a next time, she would be prepared.

Back in the room she was to occupy during the coming weeks, she finished towelling her hair dry before lying down on the bed to try and relax until dinnertime. The mountain nights might be cool, but the days were certainly warm enough. Intensified by the tin roof, the heat in here was enervating. From what she had read, if the coming season followed its normal pattern the rain would be mostly confined to the late afternoon and early evening, with storms a fairly regular occurrence. Not exactly an encouraging prospect, though thunder and lightning had never bothered her overmuch.

All part and parcel, she reflected whimsically.

She heard the hooter signalling the end of the day's work on the dot of six o'clock. Another hour until dinner. Feeling the hollowness in her stomach, she contemplated eating one of the sandwiches still standing on the tray, but they looked dry and unappetising. The remains would have to be disposed of as soon as possible. Any food left standing around could attract vermin. The one thing she did draw the line at was a rat in her room!

The site became filled with sound as the workforce returned. Feet passed her door; voices could be heard through the thin partition walls. At twenty minutes to seven, Kerry got up and put on plain black cords and a white cotton shirt. A touch of lipstick was the only feminine weakness she allowed herself. On the work site itself she probably wouldn't even bother with that. With her hair tucked up under a hard hat whenever she was called on to step outside the office, and with her body enveloped in the overalls, her femininity would soon be forgotten. She was here to learn, nothing else. Perhaps when Brad appreciated that fact he would let up on the aggravation.

Glenn knocked on her door at five minutes to the hour with an offer to escort her across to the canteen. Freshly-shaved, hair brushed into smooth obedience, he looked appealingly wholesome and reliable. In some ways he reminded her of Tim Linacre, whom she had pushed to the back of her mind.

Brad's was the first face she spotted on entering the canteen at Glenn's side. He was seated at one of the long tables on the far side of the room, deep in conversation with a couple of the other men. The spate of whistles which greeted her appearance brought the dark head up, though his face registered little expression.

So far as he was concerned, Kerry reflected, the battle was already won. He was going to have one big surprise, come the morning!

Members of the consultant team dined as a group. The meal itself proved excellent. Huge dishes of thick Irish broth were followed by steak with a whole range of accompaniments. Wedges of apple pie with custard completed the menu.

A crate of bottled beer, from which the men helped themselves, stood ready at the end of each table. Few bothered to use glasses. Kerry settled for hot coffee. She could also have had tea for the asking.

'I'm full to bursting,' she acknowledged wryly when Glenn asked if she had had enough. 'I'm going to have to watch it while I'm here, or I'll be going home looking like Tessie O'Shea!'

'No chance,' put in the man seated opposite, comfortably. 'You don't have the build for it. Me, now——' patting the pronounced bulge above his waistband '—that's a different story. Good thing my wife likes a bit of weight on a man!'

'Specially in his wallet,' riposted his neighbour. 'Hardly get through the door before mine's under a seize and search warrant! Mercenary creatures, women.' The grin directed Kerry's way took the edge off that statement. 'Present company excepted, maybe.'

She grinned back. 'Depends whether there's anything else worth taking an interest in.'

During the past forty minutes, the constraint imposed by her presence in the room appeared to have eased— in the immediate vicinity, at least. The glances cast her way were both frequent and openly appraising, but nothing to which she could take exception. She was one woman among more than forty men; obviously they were going to be interested. Once they realised she wasn't going to start carping if she happened to be in earshot of some less than refined comment they'd relax. With more and more women coming into the engineering world, they were all going to need to accustom themselves sooner or later.

'Coming over to the rec.?' asked the same man, encouraged by the retort. 'There's damned all else to do during the week.'

Aware that several others in the vicinity had overheard the question, Kerry kept her tone carefully neutral. 'I'm not sure I'd be welcome.'

The clamour of dissent which greeted the observation brought a smile to her lips again. All right, so perhaps it was the younger element who were the most enthusiastic, but it was a start. If Brad didn't like it he could do the other thing.

Surprisingly, it was Glenn who expressed doubt when they got outside. 'You're going to be under pressure,' he said. 'Some are going to take liberties.'

'Only if I let them,' she returned equably. 'If things get too hot I'll retire gracefully.'

The night air felt chill after the heat of the day. She was glad of the denim jacket about her shoulders. There had been a light shower during the last half-hour, leaving the ground sludgy under foot. It was necessary to pick one's way with care and precision in order to keep footwear reasonably dry. She still had to find out about laundry facilities, she reflected, pulling up her trouserlegs out of reach of the mud. There had to be some arrangement.

The recreation room was close by. One end contained a billiard table, with tables and chairs and a makeshift bar at the other. Beer and soft drinks only, it appeared. Spirits, Glenn said, were banned on site. The orange juice Kerry asked for was good and cold.

Good-natured ribaldry came from all sides. She took it without rancour, even scoring the occasional return hit herself. Her claim that she had played snooker before was met with male derision. It was Pete Lomas who took her up on the challenge.

With the frame set up and the watchers crowded around, she was invited to make the break. Ten minutes later, with a score of twenty-nine, she missed a shot on the blue and handed over to an opponent no longer quite so sure of himself. She lost in the end, but only by eight points: a performance which brought her admiring congratulations from an audience almost universally won over.

Pete Lomas had to spoil it, of course. 'How about a kiss for the winner?' he drawled.

'Why not?' she responded lightly, and blew him one, drawing general laughter.

'Not what I had in mind,' he said moving to block her way. There was a gleam in his eyes that signified trouble, quietening the men still standing around as they waited to see how she would handle the situation.

Brad's sudden appearance brought more dismay than relief. The only redeeming factor was that it saved Glenn from perhaps feeling the need to step in on her behalf.

'Cut it out, Lomas,' he said curtly.

The other man looked for a moment as if he might challenge the order; then he shrugged and gave way. 'Just a bit of fun.'

Like hell, Kerry thought. She made herself look Brad in the eye, her smile bland. 'You're missing the white charger!'

Grins all round greeted the sally. Brad allowed himself a faint smile. 'That was quite a show you put on,' he said. 'Supposing——'

'Want to take me on?' she asked with deliberation. 'I only just started to get warmed up.'

The steely glint was a warning in itself. 'I don't play.'

'Pity.' Her tone held regret. 'You really should learn.'

It was Glenn who broke the expectant hush as the spectators eagerly awaited the site manager's reply. He sounded uncertain. 'You didn't finish your drink, Kerry.'

'So I didn't.' She was still looking at Brad, determined not to be the first to turn away. 'Why don't you come and have one with us?'

A corner of the strong mouth turned down. 'Thanks.'

Glenn went to fetch a couple of beers, leaving Kerry to lead the way to the table they had been occupying prior to the game. The other two members of the consultant team present were too involved in some in-depth discussion even to bother looking round. With the fun over, the rest of the assembly dispersed to resume previous interests.

Seated, Brad said coolly, 'I'd watch the innuendo. It's liable to be taken at face value by some.'

Green eyes widened innocently. 'What innuendo?'

He shrugged. 'Have it your own way.' There was a pause, a change of tone. 'Did you tell him yet?'

Kerry lowered her gaze to the glass in her hand. 'Tell who what?'

He made an impatient movement. 'Stop playing games! You know what I'm talking about.'

'All right.' This time she faced him without the mask, eyes signalling defiance. 'I haven't told him because I'm not going. Is that plain enough for you?'

There was no immediate reaction. She had the feeling he had been more than half expecting the turnabout. When he did speak it was with a disquieting evenness of tone.

'You don't learn from experience.'

'I don't knuckle under to duress,' she flashed. 'Get used to it, Brad. I'm going to be around till this job is finished!'

Broad shoulders lifted. 'We'll see.'

Instinctively she borrowed his own earlier words. 'Want to take a bet on it? Forewarned, as they say, is forearmed. You won't get the opportunity to humiliate me that way again!'

His regard sharpened into mockery, sudden and disturbing. 'Is that what I did?'

'Go to hell,' she said thickly, unable to stop the telltale warmth creeping under her skin. 'Just leave me alone, Brad!'

'Or else what?'

Glenn's arrival with the beer forestalled any reply. There was really nothing left to say, Kerry conceded. She had called his bluff. End of story.

The two men began discussing some modification or other. She listened with only half an ear, mentally comparing them. More than just a difference in age and build: they were totally opposite types. Of the two of them, Glenn had to come out the winner—just as Tim would. Trustworthy, reliable, generous to a fault, that was Tim Linacre.

And dull, came the thought, creeping into her mind against all attempts to keep it out. Not his fault that he failed to stir her blood the way Brad undoubtedly did. If it came to that, nor had anyone else in the years between.

How was it, she wondered bleakly, that you could detest someone and yet be so desperately attracted to them at one and the same time? Just to sit here across from him like this made her insides curl. Resting on the edge of the table, the arm beneath the rolled sleeve of his shirt was brown and muscular, the covering of dark hair a tantalising reminder of the thick mat that grew on his chest. She remembered sliding her fingers daringly inside his shirt as he kissed her—feeling the hardness of muscle beneath the crisp curl. In that one brief week with him she had experienced emotions she would have given a fortune to recapture with someone else.

She became suddenly aware that he had stopped talking and was looking right back at her, one eyebrow slightly raised. Without haste, and hoping the heat didn't show in her face, she said casually, 'I think I'll make an early night of it.'

'I'll see you back,' Glenn offered, but she waved him down.

'I'll be fine, thanks. It's only a short distance.'

'Don't slip,' warned Brad laconically, as she got to her feet. 'It could be dangerous.'

Her smile felt stiff but her voice was level. 'I'll be careful.'

Gaining her room without mishap, she looked for a key, only to find there wasn't even a lock. Total trust, or simply a lack of anything worth stealing? she wondered. Either way, as the only woman in the place, it left her feeling vulnerable.

If she was honest, it was only Brad who presented any real threat. If he took it into his mind to slip along here during the night there was going to be very little she could do to keep him out. Both wardrobe and chest were too flimsy to present any barrier.

The noise alone, if the latter were shoved out of the way, would be deterrent enough, though, surely? she thought. Worth the effort, anyway. Telling herself he wouldn't dare try anything again was one thing, making herself believe it something else. Brad was no fool; he'd been fully aware of her response to him earlier. He wouldn't be slow to take advantage of that knowledge should the opportunity present itself again.

Before finally getting into bed, and making as little noise as possible, she pulled the chest across the front of the door. Lying in the darkness, trying to get comfortable on the thin mattress, she fought to keep her mind on thoughts appertaining to the job she was here to do. In the few weeks left she would be only marginally wiser, but every little helped. Before she committed herself to any position, she had to make some effort to straighten out her emotions where Tim was concerned, once and for all. Decisiveness was essential to the career path she had chosen to follow.

The recreation room began emptying around ten-thirty. By eleven all was quiet on camp. With a six-thirty start, a good night's sleep had to be a priority, Kerry conceded. It was gone twelve before she finally accepted that Brad wasn't going to be trying her door that night, another hour after that before she slept.

She awoke to sunlight and the clamour of a day already well under way. Rolling on to her back, she reached sleepily for the travel clock she had set on the floor at the bedside, staring in dismay at the time. Eight o'clock! It couldn't be!

The whole compound appeared deserted when she made the trip across to the ablution area. Back in her room, she pulled on jeans and a shirt and slid her feet into the same brogues she had worn yesterday, packing the overalls into a canvas bag along with the size five steel-tipped boots she had had such difficulty finding, and her hard hat. Today she would probably be spending the greater part of her time in the offices, but the gear could be left there against future occasions when she would be going out on site.

Safety consciousness had been drummed into her. Hard hats, strong footwear and a weather eye always open, that was the golden rule. If anybody managed to find her whistleworthy in that little lot, she'd be very surprised!

The smell of frying bacon was wafting across from the kitchen when she left the building. Probably Joe having a late breakfast, she thought. Her stomach was hollow, but it would have to stay that way. It was going to be near enough nine o'clock before she reached the office as it was.

With no transport available, it was necessary to walk the half-mile. A truck came rumbling up behind her as she reached the main site, the driver sounding his horn in a series of short, staccato bursts which had everybody in the vicinity looking round.

Brad was talking to a couple of the men nearby. He said something to them that drew grins before breaking away to saunter over.

'Thought you'd changed your mind,' he greeted her with irony. 'Sleep well, did you?'

'Too well,' she acknowledged with what coolness she could muster. 'Don't worry, it won't happen again.'

'Not my concern. I shouldn't imagine the boss's daughter need stick to any timetable.' He gave her no time to form a reply. 'I don't want you wandering around the site at any time on your own, is that understood?'

'Still scared I might throw a spanner in the works?' she asked caustically. 'How am I supposed to learn anything if I'm not allowed outside the office?'

'I said alone. We have a good safety record on this job. I'd as soon not spoil it. Make sure you've someone with you who knows their way around.'

She said with purpose, 'Like Pete Lomas, for instance?'

'Stick to your own side,' he advised brusquely. 'If I catch you making up to any of my men again, there'll be trouble!'

The effrontery of it took her breath away. Before she could find her voice he was moving off. Watching him go, she was seized by a strong urge to run after him and aim a kick at the seat of those close-fitting denims. Caution won by a short head. He would think nothing of returning the compliment—if only in kind. He'd been forced to accept her presence here as fact, but that didn't mean he was going to make any further concessions. She would have to watch her step every inch of the way.

Alan Pope was at his desk. He looked sceptically resigned when she proffered apologies for her lateness.

'You're not exactly a full-salaried employee,' he pointed out. 'Why should you be expected to put in the same hours as everyone else?'

'Because the discipline goes with the job,' she said. 'I realise I'll have to give you all time to clear the ablutions, but I'll be no more than twenty minutes behind you tomorrow—if I have to stay up all night to do it!'

'Bit self-defeating,' he observed. 'Anyway, what are your plans now you're here?'

Kerry looked at him a little helplessly. 'I was hoping you'd suggest where I should make a start.' Seeing the expression in his eyes, she added quickly, 'Would I be in your way if I took a look at the model over there to begin with? I've only seen drawings up to now.'

'Help yourself,' he invited, obviously relieved to have the immediate problem removed. 'I need to finish this report.'

A long table under the window contained a detailed structural model of the completed dam and surrounding terrain. She took her time studying it. The valley which was to be flooded was long and narrow, the slender, inwardly curving arch blocking off the lower end seemingly far too fragile a structure to hold back the millions of gallons of water it was designed to support. Down the escarpment, beside the diverted stream, ran the flume which would carry the water to the powerhouse.

From where she stood she could see clear across to the escarpment itself, with the dam face sheering upwards from the top of it. More than a hundred feet from the base, it was a thing of beauty in form and shape, its smooth white surface marred only by the inset sluice gates. A passenger and materials hoist was erected to one side.

The cage was ascending right now. Kerry picked up the binoculars lying to hand and adjusted the focus to bring the dam wall into close-up, following the movement to the top of the mast.

Two men got out, one of them instantly recognisable by his very build. She panned the length of his body, feeling the contraction way down deep. Strength enough there to shift mountains—enough, for sure, to have any woman helpless in his grasp. He was all male, and dangerous with it. She had to keep that fact in the forefront of her mind.

'That's done, thank God!' exclaimed Alan behind her, sitting back in his chair to ease cramped fingers. 'One job I detest is writing up the daily diary.'

Kerry replaced the binoculars and turned to look at him, tentative about making the offer yet eager to be of use. 'Do you have a pocket recorder?'

'There's one lying around somewhere,' he acknowledged. 'Taking notes that way might be quicker at the time, but I still have to write it all up in the end.'

'I could do that for you—and learn a lot about site supervision in the process.'

He looked back at her with sudden new interest. 'Now that is an idea!'

'In fact,' she added, warming to the apparent approval, 'I could do the same for everyone—if they wanted it, that is.'

'Oh, they will! Keeping records up to date is everybody's bugbear.' For the first time his smile was genuine. 'Could be you'll prove an asset, after all.'

Kerry laughed. 'Rather than a hindrance, you mean? I'll certainly do my best.'

'Just one thing,' he said. 'Try not to get across Brad Halston, will you? It's important we retain a good working relationship. A difficult man to reach on any social level,' he tagged on. 'A loner, if ever I saw one.'

Dependent on the company available, reflected Kerry, with memories of Rina Nixon. Today was Wednesday. No doubt he would be going down to see her, come the weekend. This time it would be just the two of them.

The despondency engendered by that thought was something she preferred to ignore.

With so much to learn about basic organisation, there was little opportunity to get out on site at all during the following couple of days. The consultant staff were a close-knit team without the rigid lines of demarcation Kerry had half anticipated finding. Glenn Ingram proved invaluable to her in his readiness to outline the day-to-day activities of each and every member. Site supervision couldn't be learned from books, he was fond of saying. It was necessary to spend some time with mud on your boots.

By Friday she was itching to do just that. Apart from the odd shower, the weather was beautiful, with temperatures rarely higher than the low seventies, fahrenheit.

'Another storm like the last one, and you might change your mind,' Glenn warned when she expressed her pleasure in the climate. 'Especially when it happens in the night. You'd swear the mountains were holding a free-for-all when the thunder gets going!'

Kerry laughed, refusing to be dampened. 'I'll come and hold your hand if you're scared.'

His answering smile held a certain wryness. 'You're only saying that because you think I'm safe. Bet you wouldn't make that same offer to Brad Halston.'

'I wouldn't make any offer to Brad Halston,' she returned on a shorter note, and received a shrewd glance.

'Just a joke. Rumour has it he already has a woman down in town.'

She half turned away to look out of the window. 'When do I get to go out on the site?'

He accepted the abrupt change of subject without comment. 'I need to go up top myself. Want to come?'

She turned back to look at him. 'Up top?'

'The dam wall. Got a good head for heights, have you?'

Visualising the particular height under discussion, Kerry felt her heartbeats quicken a little, but no amount of trepidation was going to make her miss out on the offer.

'Good enough,' she said. 'I'll get my things.'

On reflection, she decided to leave the white overalls where they were and settle for hard hat and boots. Accustomed to neither, she found the heaviness about feet and head both uncomfortable and ungainly.

'A real professional!' teased Glenn when she came out to join him. 'Not that anybody with half an eye is going to mistake you for one of the boys!' He indicated the Jeep standing by. 'Climb aboard.'

Skirting the welter of men and machinery hard at work in the valley bottom, they took several minutes to reach the escarpment. From this angle, the dam itself seemed to stretch to the heavens. Kerry was hard put to it to conceal the sudden shakiness in her knees as she followed Glenn into the wire cage in which they would make the ascent. She'd be OK once they were at the top, she told herself, trying not to think about coming down again. All it took was adjustment.

There was nothing smooth about that journey upwards. The whole mechanism shook and groaned as if on its last legs. As Glenn seemed unperturbed, she could only assume that this was normal, but found little comfort in the belief. When the moment finally came to step out from the cage across a gap which, though narrow, revealed a dizzy emptiness below, it was an effort to make the move.

Although broader than might have been anticipated from the model, the surface presented was far from reassuring. There was nothing to hold on to, just that sheer drop to either side of the sweeping curve.

She tried to concentrate on the far views rather than allow her gaze to drift into the depths, aware of the tingling rubbery sensation in her ankles, the drumming in her ears. It would pass. It had to pass! In the meantime no one must guess how she was feeling.

Seeing Brad moving forward to meet them was a blow. She should have realised, of course, that he would naturally be involved in any query Glenn had to make. It took every ounce of will-power she had to wipe all trace of panic from her eyes as she met his gaze.

He made no comment regarding her presence, turning his attention to the drawing Glenn was unrolling. Standing there at the latter's side, she tried to follow the point he was making—to evaluate Brad's argument in return. Much of it, she had to confess, was over her head, but what she did manage to retain was filed away in her mind for the moment when she could relate the detail to that outlined in her reference books. What she should have done, she acknowledged ruefully, was to have brought a notebook of her own with her.

Engrossed in the discussion, she managed to forget her surroundings. Only when both men started moving out along the top of the dam to look at some further detail did she return to full awareness.

She forced herself to follow them, keeping her eyes fixed on Brad's back. When they paused they were right on the edge overlooking the dam interior. Not quite as deep on this side, admittedly, but high enough to make her head start spinning again.

Try as she might, she couldn't stop herself from looking down into the gorge. A shaft of sunlight made the white water of the river sparkle as it tumbled over its rocky bed far below. The drumming in her ears became a crescendo; she felt as if something were drawing her down into those depths. It would be so easy just to let herself go. All she had to do was lean into the void . . .

CHAPTER FIVE

VAGUELY, as if from some far distance, Kerry heard a shout, then a hand was clamped on her shoulder, dragging her back even as she teetered on the brink of oblivion.

'What the hell do you think you're doing?' grated Brad's voice in her ear. 'You were nearly over the damned edge!' His expression underwent an abrupt alteration as he looked at her white face. 'We'll sort this out later,' he clipped over his shoulder to Glenn.

'I'll be all right in a minute,' she protested weakly. 'I just went a bit dizzy, that's all.'

'Vertigo,' he said. 'The last thing you need up here!'

'I'll take her down.' Glenn's initial bewilderment had turned to concern, mingled with apology. 'I'm sorry, Kerry. I didn't realise.'

'It isn't your fault,' she murmured. 'I didn't realise myself.' She met grey eyes, summoning a shaky smile. 'I'm fine now.'

'Going to take the hoist?' Brad asked, ignoring the assurance. His lip curled ironically at the involuntary leap of panic in her eyes. 'I came up via the road,' he said. 'Think you can make it that far without passing out—or shall I carry you?'

From where they stood to where the dam crest met solid rock was no great distance, but to Kerry, right now, even a couple of feet was too much. It was pride alone that brought her head up.

'I'll walk, thanks.' She turned the smile in Glenn's direction. 'See you back at the office.'

Even with Brad right at her side, it took everything she had to make that short journey. The road broadened into a turning circle at the dam head. Several vehicles were parked there, among them the Land Rover to which Brad led the way. He put her into the front passenger seat before going round to slide behind the wheel.

'I suppose,' she said tightly as he put the car into motion, 'this gives you another reason to carp about my being here!'

'I don't need another reason,' came the brusque reply. 'All it's done is underline my initial one. On a job like this you're a liability.'

'I can't be the first to suffer a mild attack of vertigo,' she protested. 'Men aren't born with a natural immunity!'

'The ones who aren't don't go in for this type of job. Probably because they *are* born with more sense.' There was no give in him at all. 'Your father has a lot to answer for in letting you near the place!'

'My father,' she said through clenched teeth, 'considers me capable of choosing my own path.'

'Even if you kill yourself doing it?'

'That's an exaggeration, and you know it!'

'Do I?' He shot her a glance, taking in the lack of colour yet in her face with a fresh tautening of his jawline. 'The only reason you're not lying down there in that river is because one of the men spotted what was happening.'

'Enabling you to play the rescuing angel again!' The flippancy was deliberate. 'How can I ever thank you?'

He smiled thinly. 'Stick around and you'll find out.'

'Not that again!' She made no attempt to conceal the scorn. 'There's nothing you can say or do that will make me pack my bags, Brad. I was in no real danger up there. All I needed was time to adjust.'

A buttress of rock hid the valley from view for several hundred yards. He drew the Land Rover to a jerky standstill, sitting for a long moment with his forearms resting on the wheel as he studied her. Kerry gazed back at him defiantly, paying no heed to the hammering of her heart.

His face looked almost as hard as the hat on his head. Every line of it was scorched into her memory. She felt an almost irresistible urge to put out her hand and touch the firm lips—to feel them soften beneath her fingers; to part and clasp. He had taught her so much four years ago, and yet so little. Her whole body ached for that further knowledge.

'I have to get back to the office,' she said, and knew her voice was pitched too high. 'If you don't...'

He seemed to reach out almost in slow motion, taking off her hat at the same time as his own, and slinging both into the rear of the cab. The hand at the back of her neck felt like hot steel, his mouth a force she couldn't resist. Without even thinking about it, she opened her lips to him, moving forward on the seat to bring herself closer, feeling the crushing strength in his arms as he drew her the rest of the way.

She couldn't even find it in herself to struggle when he unfastened her shirt buttons and slid a hand inside; she wanted his touch. At the very back of her mind was the recognition of regret to come, but that was later and this was now.

Her brassière yielded to his seeking fingers, baring her breasts to the hand he knew so well how to use. A moan was dragged from deep down in her throat to be stifled against his lips. He was so big, so hard, so totally and implacably male.

It took the movement of that same hand down to the waistband of her jeans to bring her to her senses. Quivering, she tried to thrust herself away from him, brought up short by his refusal to release her.

'What's the problem?' he asked grimly. 'Isn't this what you were angling for?'

'Angling?' She could scarcely get the word out through the sudden searing rejection. Her eyes blazed as the truth struck home. 'You bastard, Brad!'

'That's twice.' He caught the fist she aimed at his face, holding it in a grip of iron. 'It still isn't too late to give you the hiding you should have had years ago,' he threatened. 'Believe me, I'd enjoy doing it!'

She did believe him. He was capable, she thought bitterly, of anything. She sank back into her seat as he let go of the hand, resisting the urge to rub crushed knuckles. Hatred was too mild a word to describe what she felt at this moment. Had she had a weapon to hand, she would have known no compunction, she was sure, in using it.

'Is there any limit to the depths you'll stoop to?' she demanded contemptuously.

His eyes registered a fresh spark. 'Depends on the provocation. Next time there won't be any stopping.' He restarted the engine with a flick of a strong, tanned wrist, rightly assured there would be no retort forthcoming. 'Stay at ground level in future. We're not running a nursery service.'

There was no answer she could give to that, either— or none that she cared to risk. She felt sick at the thought of how far she had allowed herself to be used.

Her shirt still hung open. She fastened the buttons with fingers that felt nerveless, uncomfortable in the loosened brassière. If she pulled out her shirt at the back she could reach the clip to refasten it, but she lacked the insouciance to do it in Brad's presence. She would simply have to rely on finding a quiet corner to make repairs before she went back into the office.

She was nonplussed when he carried straight on past the building.

'It's only a couple of hours or so till finishing time,' he said before she could comment. 'You won't be expected back after Glenn explains what happened.'

'It isn't up to you to decide,' she retorted furiously. 'Just stop this damned thing!'

He ignored the injunction. Short of jumping from the vehicle, there was little she could do but go along. Anger created a white-hot spot in the centre of her chest. Who the devil did he think he was?

'Just as a matter of interest,' she said with icy control, when he brought the Land Rover to a stop outside the staff quarters, 'I left my shoes back in the office. Are you prepared to fetch them for me?'

'I doubt if you only brought the one pair,' he returned drily. 'Anyway, the boots are pretty fetching.' He got out of the car to open the outer door, standing back with mock gallantry to allow her entry. 'You'll feel better after a rest.'

She passed him with some trepidation, half anticipating an intention to follow her in. There was a sense too dangerously close to disappointment when he let the door swing closed again with him still on the outside. Would she never learn?

Reaction set in the moment she was alone in the claustrophobic little room. If Brad hadn't grabbed her up there she would have gone over. She had suffered vertigo before, but only in a mild form. On the other hand, she had never been that high before without some kind of protection.

Not that she was going to let this episode put her off, she thought resolutely. Fear could be conquered. All it took was perseverance.

It was her feelings for Brad that were beginning to be the real problem. Her body reacted to him regardless of what her mind was telling her. Perhaps the worst part was that he had no real interest in her as a woman. He was simply out to teach her a lesson. Avoiding him altogether was going to be difficult, but she could at least make sure she was never alone with him again. She *had* to make sure.

She gave it ten minutes or so before leaving. Glenn was back in the office when she got there. He looked surprised to see her.

'Brad indicated you were feeling too shaken to come back in,' he said. 'Are you sure you're OK?'

'I'm fine,' Kerry assured him. 'Brad made far too much of it.' She kept her tone casual. 'There's no need for anyone else to know, is there?'

'Sorry,' he said ruefully. 'Alan was in here when Brad dropped by. He's given strict orders that you're not to go on top again.'

'That's hardly fair,' she protested. 'I can't spend my whole life at ground level just because of one incident! The only way I'm going to overcome it is by experience.'

'I realise that.' Glenn's tone was sympathetic. 'If it's any comfort, I suffered the same kind of reaction the first time I went up on a structure.'

'Were *you* grounded?' she asked.

'No,' he admitted. 'But——'

'Which means I'm being penalised simply because I happen to be female!' Her voice had risen; she could see heads lifting beyond the glass partitions—Alan Pope's included. 'This needs straightening out,' she added on a quieter note. 'And there's no time like the present!'

The resident engineer was waiting for her. He listened to what she had to say with apparent patience, but there was nothing undecided about the shake of his head when she finished.

'As your father's representative on site, I owe it to him to ensure the safety of each and every member of the staff,' he declared. 'How do you think he'd feel if his only daughter lost her life falling off the top of a dam being built under his supervision?'

The gold in her hair caught the light as her head moved in rejoinder. 'It won't happen again.'

'That's right, it won't. Because there isn't going to be an opportunity.' He held up a staying hand as she opened her mouth to argue further. 'I'm sorry, Kerry, but that's the way it is.'

'I can't conquer the problem without facing it,' she said, forcing a reasonable tone. 'It's like being thrown from a horse. The only way is to get right back on again.'

He said drily, 'You wouldn't be picking yourself up from a hundred and ten feet. With regard to future jobs, that would be up to the resident in charge. With regard to this one, the answer is still no.'

'You share Brad Halston's attitude, don't you?' she accused. 'You don't think women have any place in this precious little world of yours!'

'I try to keep an open mind on the subject,' he rejoined. 'You're not making it any easier right now.'

Kerry bit her lip. Arguing the toss was getting her no-where, yet simply to accept the situation went against the grain. Compromise was the only immediate solution.

'You're the boss,' she said.

She spent the rest of the afternoon studying drawing revisions. Wisely Glenn left her alone. Only when they were on the way back to the camp did he say mildly, 'It isn't the end of the world, you know.'

Her smile was brief. 'I sometimes feel as if I'm batting my head against a brick wall!'

'Minorities always have a struggle,' he observed. 'There are plenty of ways you can prove yourself without having to walk a tightrope.'

She had to laugh. 'Some tightrope!'

'A matter of perspective.' He paused, tone altering. 'You're a very special kind of person, Kerry. There can't be all that many girls in the business who'd put up with the conditions you're putting up with.'

The note in his voice made her suddenly wary. Much as she liked Glenn, she had no desire for any personal involvement. 'My fiancé thinks I'm mad, too,' she responded lightly, and knew her instincts hadn't been wrong when his expression changed.

'I didn't know you were engaged,' he said. 'You don't wear a ring.'

'Hardly the place *to* wear one, is it?'

They were already turning on to the camp site, bumping over the ruts left by some other, heavier vehicle. He waited until he drew up outside the hut before saying curiously, 'Doesn't your fiancé mind not seeing you for weeks on end?'

'He's an engineer, too,' she said, as if that were answer enough. 'Thanks for the lift, Glenn. See you in the canteen.'

Tim minded all right, she thought wryly, heading indoors. Her insistence on coming here had been the cause of their first real row. Just because he had chosen design as his métier, it wasn't to say her ambitions had to follow a similar track. She wanted to be right out there with the job—seeing the dream transmuted into actuality. If he couldn't appreciate that, then they might as well call it a day.

Alan Pope's ban stuck in her craw still, but she couldn't allow it too much importance. Site supervision was a craft in itself. She would have her work cut out imbibing the basic principles alone, to say nothing of the practicalities.

Catching Brad's mocking smile across the canteen later did nothing to enhance her view of the afternoon's events. If it hadn't been for him, Alan need never have known of the incident. Glenn could almost certainly have been prevailed upon to keep his own counsel.

She became suddenly aware that the latter was speaking to her, turning on an apologetic smile as she brought her attention to bear.

'Sorry, I was miles away. What did you say?'

'I was asking what you intended doing at the weekend,' he repeated. 'Las Meridas isn't exactly a Mecca of entertainment, but there's usually something going on. The Mexicans have more *fiestas* than they do hot dinners!'

Kerry laughed. 'Sounds promising. Work finishes early on Saturdays, doesn't it?'

'Twelve-thirty,' he confirmed. 'There's a skeleton staff left on site by rota. The rest are away by half-past one.' He hesitated, not looking at her. 'If you want company, I've no particular plans myself. No strings attached, of course.'

She would have preferred to keep her options open, Kerry thought, but she couldn't bring herself to turn the offer down. 'Thanks,' she said lightly. 'I could do with some back-up when I go to tell Miguel about his car. I don't imagine he's going to be over the moon about it.'

Glenn shook his head. 'He doesn't have a leg to stand on.'

The evening passed as all other evenings. Boredom had to play a large part in any contract of this nature, Kerry judged, overhearing an altercation between a couple of the men over some minor disagreement. The weekends were by way of being a safety valve. Without that opportunity to let off steam, the whole camp would probably erupt.

'Fancy a game tonight?' asked a too-familiar voice, and she turned her head to see Pete Lomas looming over her. The over-confident blue eyes travelled from her face down to the thrust of her breasts against the material of her shirt, lingering there for a deliberate moment or two before lifting again. 'I've been practising.'

'I'm not in the mood,' she said briefly. 'Why don't you ask someone else?'

He laughed. 'Scared of losing again? I'll give you a twenty-point start.'

She kept her tone light and level. 'Thanks, but no thanks.'

The smile disappeared, his expression turning ugly. 'Saving it all for your own crowd?'

'That's enough of that!' Glenn was on his feet, eyes blazing, hands balling into fists. 'Take off, Lomas!'

The other man sneered. 'Want to see me off?'

Kerry put her hand on Glenn's arm as he made a jerky move. His opponent was both taller and heavier, and almost certainly lacking in the finer points of sportsmanship. She said bitingly, 'Go paddle your canoe up some other creek, Mr Lomas!'

The burst of laughter from those close enough to overhear was hardly designed to improve matters. Pete looked fit to do someone an injury.

'You heard the lady,' somebody drawled. 'Go cool off, man.'

Kerry let out her pent-up breath in a sigh of relief when he turned on his heel. Making the man look a fool had been no way to handle the situation. Incidents like that one would be fuel to Brad's objections. She could only be thankful that he wasn't present—although no doubt he'd hear about it, and with embellishments.

Glenn sat down again. He looked a bit sheepish. 'You shouldn't have stopped me,' he murmured.

'His kind wouldn't know a fair fight if he saw one,' she returned. 'In any case, I don't want anybody fighting over me. I came prepared to take anything this job could throw up. Loudmouths like Pete Lomas don't merit a second thought!'

'I don't think he'll be prepared to just forget it,' he said. 'You'll need to watch out for him.'

'I'll do that.' She stirred restlessly. 'I think I'll turn in. I want to write a couple of letters to put in the post tomorrow.'

'I'll see you back,' Glenn offered, but she shook her head.

'I don't need nursemaiding, thanks. You stay and finish your drink.'

It had rained pretty heavily earlier. Judging from the amount of cloud still hanging around, there could well be more to come. Duckboards had been laid between the main buildings, which made things easier. She paused to allow her sight to adjust to night vision before stepping out on them, aware that a slip could land her in mud up to her ankles.

She was passing the first of the dormitory huts when she heard the footsteps behind her. An arm snaked about her waist, half lifting her from the ground, the hand covering her mouth stifling her involuntary cry. It had to be Pete Lomas, she thought in consternation, struggling to free herself as she was carried into the shadow of the hut. He must have followed her when she left!

He set her down with her back against the wooden wall, trapping her there with the weight of his body, the hand still over her mouth.

'Yell, and I'll hurt you!' he threatened. 'We've got some sorting out to do.' He took the hand away only to lay his forearm across her throat, his expression gloating as he saw the flash of fear in her eyes. 'Different now, isn't it? Just you and me, babe. How'd you like it?'

'This is stupid,' she said thickly. 'How do you think you're going to get away with it?'

The arm tautened on her throat, making her gag. 'Who gives a damn? You've been asking for it all week.'

'All I've done,' she forced out, 'is be here.'

'Right enough. One female among forty men. Think I'm the only one with ideas?' His laugh was low and coarse. 'You should hear some of the others talking about what they'd like to do to you!'

'Talk's cheap,' she gritted. 'What you're contemplating is another thing altogether!'

The laugh came again. 'You don't know what I've got in mind yet. For starters though...' His free hand came up to cover her breast, the exploration lacking any gentleness. 'Nice,' he mouthed approvingly. 'Like that, don't you? Bints like you want it rough. Well, you got it, babe! Let's have this shirt off.'

His hold on her relaxed a fraction as he ripped at the buttons. Kerry brought up her knee with all the force she could summon behind it, hearing his agonised intake of breath as she connected. He staggered away from her, hands clutching his groin, a low keening sound coming from his lips.

'Nice,' said Brad drily, moving into view around the corner of the hut. 'That should settle him down for a day or two.'

Her own breath coming in short fast gulps, Kerry stared at the tall, dark figure.

'You've been standing there watching!' she accused.

'Not watching,' he rejoined. 'Listening. I saw him follow you out of the rec.'

'Why didn't you stop him?'

Broad shoulders lifted. 'I thought you should have a chance to handle it yourself. There won't always be somebody around to get you out of trouble.'

'You did it purposely,' she accused. 'In fact, I wouldn't put it past you to have set the whole thing up!'

'I might have if I hadn't been pretty sure it was going to happen anyway, sooner or later.' He moved to where the other man was still bent double, pulling him upright by the scruff of his neck to look into the livid features. 'That was your one bite, Lomas. Right?'

There was a throttled mutter which could have been agreement. Brad obviously took it as such because he let him go. Still standing with the hut wall at her back, Kerry watched her assailant move off painfully into the night.

'You're not going to do anything?' she asked unbelievingly. 'That man was threatening rape!'

There was irony in the line of his mouth. 'Talk's cheap, remember? I don't imagine there's a man on site who hasn't fantasised about having you in bed with him at nights. With most of them that's as far as it will go. Lomas is one of the exceptions.'

'So fire him!' she snapped.

The shrug came again. 'Why should I deprive a man of his job because he gives way to a passing temptation? I don't have any complaints about his work.'

'It wasn't a spur-of-the-moment idea,' she argued with heat. 'He already...' Her voice died away at the look in the grey eyes.

'Already what?'

She shook her head. 'It isn't important now.'

'I'll be the judge of that.' He loomed over her, too close for comfort. 'Give!'

'He was annoyed because I refused to play snooker with him,' she said reluctantly. 'He made some rather suggestive remarks, that's all.'

'So you took the huff and headed for home, is that it?'

'Not quite like that, no.' Her chin was up, her eyes signalling resentment. 'I felt like an early night.'

'Leaving on your own with Lomas hot on your trail!' Brad's tone would have cut steel. 'I'd say you asked for all you got!'

'You would, wouldn't you?' Tears of anger and frustration threatened her pride. She blinked them back furiously. 'If I hadn't kneed him in the groin, you'd have probably let him carry on, just to prove a point. That's the kind of swine you are!'

It was too dark to see his features all that clearly, but his posture, though unchanged, had stiffened. When he spoke it was with a clipped quietness far more dangerous than if he had ranted and raved. 'If that's your opinion, I'd as soon not disappoint you.'

The hand fastening on her upper arm was hard enough to hurt. Dragged along at his side, she fought to keep her footing in the clinging mud. It was obvious where he was taking her. The only place to go was her room.

CHAPTER SIX

BRAD'S own room came first; Kerry had forgotten that. Shoving her inside, he shut the door with a purposeful thud, not bothering to switch on the bare bulb overhead.

Kerry passed the tip of her tongue over dry lips as she stared at him. 'I'll raise the roof before I let you touch me!' she got out.

'They're all over in the rec. We're on our own for at least another hour.' He paused, his regard unrelenting. 'Would you rather I fetched Lomas back?'

'I'd rather you just went!'

'This is my room,' he pointed out.

'Then *I'll* go.' She made a move towards the door, brought up short by his failure to stand back from it. 'Brad,' she began desperately, 'this is——'

'It's time somebody taught you something about human nature,' he said hardily. 'Better coming from me than friend Lomas.'

'Where's the difference?' she flashed, losing all restraint in the sudden rush of anger. 'You're neither of you fit to be called men!'

His laugh held a certain grim humour. 'There's one qualification you're about to experience.'

'Stop it!' She could hardly speak through the pain in her throat. 'Just stop it, will you? You've gone far enough.'

'Not nearly,' he said. 'You've had this coming for too long. I should have carried it through the other night. You might have got the message then.'

She put out a futile hand to ward him off as he moved to take hold of her. The sudden clap of thunder seemingly right overhead jerked every nerve in her body. Rain followed like a cloudburst. If there had been any chance at all of anyone making an early return, it was gone now. Until this finished, they were isolated.

His mouth was punishing. She felt stifled under it, all the power drained from her limbs. Pete Lomas had already ripped several of the buttons from her shirt. Brad completed the job, stripping the garment from her with a ruthlessness that froze her heart.

She made a feeble attempt to stop him taking off her brassière, but it was a wasted effort. Her whole body stiffened as he dropped his head to her breast, her back arching involuntarily to the agonising sensation. The slow, circling movement of his tongue was like fire on her skin. Her hands came up to fasten in his hair, the will to tug him away ebbing by the moment. A steadily growing heat spread through her body, curling tendrils into every extremity.

She trembled at the touch of his hands at her waist— the unbuckling of her belt, the sliding of the zip. The taut material was pushed down over her thighs, sliding of its own momentum down to her ankles. He lifted her up to pull off her muddy shoes along with the jeans, tossing the whole bundle into a corner before standing back to start taking off his own clothing.

Quivering, she watched him, incapable now of protest. His body was all she had anticipated: the muscle smoothly defined beneath tanned skin, shoulders tapering down to narrow waist and hips...the thrusting manhood. The quivering became a trembling, starting deep in the pit of her belly. She had once seen a mare displaying these same symptoms as the stallion was

brought to her; for the first time she could fully appreciate the animal's feelings. Fear was a part of it, but only
a part. Desire was a gathering force, sweeping all before
it.

Not like the other night, she thought blindly as he
pressed her down on to the bed. This time she was going
to know him through and through. She had wanted him
this way four years ago, although the need then had been
nothing compared with what she was experiencing now.

Kneeling over her, he ran both hands slowly over her
body, following every line, every curve, making her
pulses race so hard and fast she thought they would jump
right out from under her skin.

She slid her hands over the broad shoulders as he
lowered himself to trace out the same lines with his
mouth, feeling the muscle ripple beneath her fingertips;
sensing the power he was holding in check. Her flimsy
briefs had already been removed; she wasn't sure at which
point. Her abdomen fluttered to the lingering caress of
his lips, her muscles tensing like highly strung wires.

When he parted her thighs at last she was ready for
him, moving in tune with him, the world spinning faster
and faster until it tilted on its axis, the cry torn from
her lips echoed by the thunder still rolling overhead.

He stayed with her afterwards, weight supported on
his elbows. His breathing was heavy, his head bent so
that all she could see was his hair and brows. Nothing
had ever prepared her for the exquisite pleasure she had
just experienced, she thought mistily. He had taken her
into another dimension.

Her emotions were so mixed it was impossible to sort
them. There was so much about him she hated, and yet
he could do this to her. It was what she had wanted from
the moment she had laid eyes on him again; she could

admit that at last. There had never been anyone else who could arouse the same overriding passion. To lie here now, pinioned beneath him, was the ultimate in sheer gratification. She wished they could stay like this forever.

It was like being torn in two when he pulled away from her. It was difficult to see his expression as he sat up to reach for his clothes; the darkness was too intense.

He made a gesture of dissent when she started to form his name. 'I think it's all been said, don't you? Let's leave it at that.'

Whatever her emotions of a moment ago, the only feeling she had now was blind, searing rage. She sat up herself, heedless of her nudity, to bring her clenched fist down hard on the back of his neck.

'Bastard!' she screamed at him.

He twisted to seize her flailing arms and pin her down to the mattress again, holding her there with grim purpose, the glitter in his eyes discernible even in the darkness.

'Cut it out,' he grated, 'or I'll give you something to really get het up about.'

'You used me,' she accused bitterly. 'There's no name I could call you that would even come close to describing what you are!'

'I did what you asked me to do four years ago,' he said. 'On the face of it, I'd say you enjoyed it a great deal more now than you would have done then.' There was a pause, a change of tone. 'For God's sake, what did you expect? You goaded me into it.'

'Man's age-old excuse!'

His lips twisted. 'OK, so I took advantage. If it hadn't happened tonight it would have happened another night. You wanted it as much as I did.'

'That's not true!' She struggled to free herself from his grasp, desisting abruptly as his fingers tightened on her arm. 'You're hurting me!'

'Not half as much as you need,' he said grimly. 'You put yourself in the way of all this. I'd as soon not have laid eyes on you again.' He drew in a heavy breath, letting go of her to sit back and run impatient fingers through his hair. 'Do you have any idea what the sight of you can do to a man out here? The outfits you wear don't help any. It would take a tent to hide that shape!'

'I can't help the way I look.' Her voice was low and ragged. 'And I've no intention of giving up on what I want to do just because a bunch of men happen to find it difficult to control so-called natural impulses. I handled Lomas. I'll do the same with anybody else who tries the same thing.'

The dark head turned, irony in the line of his mouth. 'How come I got lucky?'

It took a real effort to level her tone. 'Sexual need isn't a male prerogative. Maybe if Pete Lomas had shown a little more finesse, he might have pipped you to the post!'

His eyes narrowed. 'Say that again.'

'You heard.' The blood was drumming in her ears, but she wasn't about to let caution in on the act now. 'There's little enough to choose between the pair of you when it comes right down to it!'

There was a heart-stopping moment when she thought he was going to grab her again, but he brought himself up short. Getting up, he dragged her roughly to her feet, turning her towards the door.

'You'd better get back to your own room,' he growled. 'And sharpish!'

'Like this?' she protested.

He let go of her to scoop her clothing from the floor where he had tossed it, pushing the bundle into her arms. His face was set like stone. 'Now take off!'

With the only other choice to insist on getting dressed again under his eyes, it was no contest, Kerry decided bleakly. At least she wouldn't be running into anyone else with the rain still coming down the way it was.

She hesitated at the door, glancing back to see him still standing there, outlined against the slightly paler square that was the window. Swallowing, she began, 'Brad, I——'

'If you don't get out of here,' he said in measured tones, 'I'm going to beat the hell out of you!'

He meant it; there was no doubting that. Chin jutting, she left the room, closing the door softly behind her. Her own room was mere yards away, but it seemed miles. Stumbling inside, she stood for a moment with her back against the door feeling the misery well up in her throat. Everything was in such a mess—including her emotions. Brad had made love to her at last, and it meant nothing. Not to him. They were further apart now than they had ever been.

Partly her own fault, she had to admit. She should never have made that comparison. Brad hadn't taken her against her will. He'd known as well as she did that her protests had been meaningless. Facing him again was going to be difficult, but it had to be done. Not even this was going to drive her away.

Almost every available vehicle was commandeered for the journey down to Las Meridas on Saturday afternoon. Dressed in their best, laughing and joking and generally giving the impression of school let out for the day, the site crew packed into a couple of the larger trucks.

Glenn had the use of a Land Rover. Seated at his side as they headed out of the valley in the wake of the trucks, Kerry could scarcely believe it was less than a week since her arrival. She had seen nothing at all of Brad this morning. He seemed to have disappeared off the face of the earth. Swallowed up by the devil, with any luck, she thought grimly.

She had hardly slept last night, unable to stop her mind endlessly circling. Forgetting was impossible when her whole body ached this way. What she had to do was learn to live with the knowledge of her own weakness where Brad was concerned.

After last night's storm, the road was littered with debris, although all vehicles in use had enough clearance to get through without difficulty. Last weekend there had been a landslide that hadn't been cleared until the Sunday, Glenn advised. The rockfall she had run into must have been the tail-end of it.

There seemed to be a whole crowd of people waiting in the small plaza on the edge of the town. Many of them were female, Kerry noted. They greeted the men jumping down from the trucks with cries of welcome.

'The town's ladies of easy virtue,' said Glenn with a rather quaint turn of phrase. 'They make sure all pockets are cleaned out before the weekend is over.'

Kerry looked at him with lifted brows. 'You mean they spend all they earn?'

He shook his head. 'KDC pay a set amount of salary into an offshore bank. Makes sure they have something to go home to.' He started to edge the Land Rover forward again as the crowd began to diminish. 'Miguel first, wouldn't you say?'

'Kerry!' The hail came from some short distance away. 'Wait a minute!'

Kerry twisted in her seat to see Rina Nixon pushing her way through the throng. The American woman was alone, her blonde hair a beacon among so many dark heads. She ignored the whistles and catcalls from a small group of men still as yet undecided on their plan of campaign.

'Glad I caught you,' she said on reaching the car. 'Brad thought it might be a good idea if you stayed at my place tonight.'

Kerry looked back at her in confusion for a moment. 'Why?'

Rina shrugged. 'Concern for your safety, I guess. Things can get a bit rough up there Saturday nights.' Her glance shifted to Glenn. 'True?'

His hesitation was brief. 'One or two might have a bit too much,' he admitted. 'Brad usually manages to keep the lid on.'

'Except that he isn't going to be there tonight,' she said. 'He has business in Ciudad.'

So Brad wasn't in the habit of spending the night down here with Rina, Kerry reflected. Not that that meant there was nothing between them, after all. 'It's good of you to offer,' she said, 'but I don't really see the necessity.'

'I don't know,' said Glenn doubtfully. 'There's never been a woman on camp before. Somebody might get ideas.'

'I didn't bring anything with me.'

'I can supply whatever you need.' Rina was taking her acceptance for granted. 'Look, do whatever you have to do, then come on up for supper. You're welcome to come, too,' she added to Glenn.

'Thanks.' He sounded agreeably surprised. 'A couple of hours, then?'

'Fine.' She stood back. 'See you then.'

'It might be nice,' Kerry remarked caustically as they moved off, 'if I were allowed to make my own decisions.'

Glenn gave her a swift glance, his expression crestfallen. 'I thought it seemed a good idea, that's all. Might have been better if Brad had mentioned it to you first, but it perhaps only occurred to him at the last minute.' He paused briefly. 'She seems OK.'

Kerry gave vent to a sudden wry sigh. 'I didn't even introduce you, did I? Sorry, Glenn. Her name is Rina Nixon. She's an artist spending a few months working in the area. I stayed at her place on Monday night after flying in from Monterrey.'

'That must have been the same flight Brad came in on himself.'

'Yes, it was.' She made no attempt to add to that statement. 'Do you really think it necessary for me to stay in town tonight.'

'Safer,' he qualified. 'I'd have thought you'd leap at the chance. Facilities have to be better than up at the camp.' He waited a moment before adding tentatively, 'Is it because Brad suggested it?'

'I don't like him interfering in something that's no business of his,' she returned. 'He takes too much on himself!'

'Strictly speaking, it *is* his business. He may not approve of having a woman on camp, but he wouldn't want anything untoward happening to you.'

Only, she thought with cynicism, if he was the perpetrator! Aloud, she said, 'You're probably right—I'm just being bolshie. Forget it, Glenn. Let's get the car business sorted out.'

They found the garage owner in his office. From the shifty look in his eyes when he saw her, Kerry had a strong suspicion that he already knew of the car's fate. His reaction on hearing the story was entirely predictable. The vehicle must be paid for, he declared, suddenly developing an ability to both speak and understand the English language. She had taken out no insurance against the loss.

It was useless for Kerry to point out she had been offered no insurance. The car hadn't been worth insuring, and they both knew it. Glenn tried reasoning with the man, and then getting angry, but to no avail. If she didn't pay the exorbitant figure demanded by Monday, Kerry gathered, the police would be informed.

'I don't think he'll take it that far,' Glenn observed when they finally left the garage. 'You could always get him for leasing you a car that wasn't even fit to be on the road in the first place.'

'Except that the evidence is at the bottom of a gully,' Kerry pointed out ruefully. 'Who can tell how the police here are going to react, anyway? I don't want to finish up in some Mexican prison cell.'

'You mean you're going to pay?'

'Seems I may have to. I'll need to wire home for the money, though. I didn't bring nearly enough with me.' She attempted a more cheerful note. 'You must know the town quite well by now. Supposing you give me a guided tour before supper?'

Taking his cue, Glenn left the subject alone, although it was obvious that he found his own failure to sort matters out for her somewhat mortifying. Kerry tried to keep the notion that Brad would have had more success from surfacing. Glenn had done his best. It wasn't his fault that she was landed with this problem in the first place.

As in most Mexican towns or villages, no matter what size, the church was magnificent, more like a cathedral with its lofty pillars and soaring arches and superbly illustrative wall-paintings. The contrast with many of the dwellings along the narrow back-streets outside was ludicrous, Kerry thought, but hopefully all that would change as the town extended.

The market vendors were still doing good business in the plaza. On impulse, she bought one of the full tiered skirts in brilliant colours, together with a white drawstring blouse that could be worn either on or off the shoulder as fancy dictated. A pair of light leather sandals completed the outfit.

'If I'm not going back to camp, I might as well take the opportunity to relax in something feminine,' she told Glenn lightly.

They got to Rina's house around six-thirty. This time Kerry performed proper introductions, apologising for her earlier lack of appreciation.

'It just doesn't seem right that you should have to be put out this way,' she said by way of excuse. 'Brad shouldn't have asked it of you.'

'Nice to have the company,' came the mild response. 'Same room as last time, if you want to take those up.' She was eyeing the unwrapped bundle in Kerry's hands. Then she smiled at Glenn. 'Sit down and have a drink.'

The two of them were chatting away like old friends when Kerry eventually came down again, wearing the skirt and blouse. Glenn looked at her appreciatively.

'You'd certainly better not wear *that* up there,' he agreed.

'You can always leave them here,' Rina offered. 'A pity you didn't bring your laundry down with you. I don't imagine facilities are all that good on site?'

'I manage, thanks.' Kerry forbore to mention that she washed her things through under the shower. She took a seat at Glenn's side on one of the sofas, accepting the glass of wine already poured for her. 'You said Brad had business in Ciudad?' she asked casually.

'That's right. He came through quite early this morning.'

And stayed how long? Kerry wondered. The fact that he had made love to her last night wouldn't bother him; the motivation had hardly been the same. The question was, would Rina take quite the same liberal view of the matter? Not that she had any intention of telling her. She couldn't bring herself to inflict that kind of hurt on anyone.

The evening was a success, she supposed, so far as it went. Glenn certainly seemed to enjoy having two women to himself. It was with obvious reluctance that he finally took his leave.

'It's been a real treat,' he said to Rina. 'A nice change from sitting around in some *cantina*.'

'You're welcome,' she responded easily. 'Hope you don't run into any trouble on the way back.'

Kerry accompanied him to the door. 'Thanks for everything, Glenn,' she said with genuine warmth.

'Only sorry I couldn't get Miguel to back down,' he apologised ruefully. 'Although I still don't think the police would take any action. Why don't you ask Rina for her opinion? She might have a better idea.'

'I'll think about it,' she promised.

He left it at that. 'You'll need transport back tomorrow,' he said. 'If I pick you up mid-afternoon, we could finish looking round the town and have a meal at a restaurant.'

'That sounds fine,' she agreed, seeing no other way open to her, short of joining the crew on the trucks. 'About three, then? And thanks again.'

Rina gave her a quizzical glance when she returned to the lamplit room. 'I guess you made a conquest there,' she observed. 'Nice guy.'

'Very,' Kerry agreed, and drew a smile.

'Not your type? No, I didn't think so. There's no challenge in Mr Nice Guy.'

'The only reason I'm not interested in Glenn that way,' Kerry replied with deliberation, 'is because I'm already engaged to be married to someone else. As a matter of fact, he's rather like Glenn.'

'Really?' Rina had an odd expression in her eyes. 'You never mentioned a fiancé last week.'

'It just didn't come up. And, before you ask, I don't wear a ring because we decided not to make it official until I get back home.'

Blonde brows lifted. 'I wasn't going to ask. Plenty of folks don't bother with a ring these days.' She paused, eyeing the contents of the coffee-cup in her hand. 'Does Brad know?'

'I don't have any reason to tell him.' She added with intent, 'If you want the truth, I'm sick to the back teeth of Brad Halston.'

'He's the kind of man who elicits strong feelings,' came the smooth rejoinder. 'Would you like some more wine?'

Was that a simple observation? Kerry wondered. Or was she being ever so subtly warned off? If the latter, Rina had no cause for alarm. Brad's initial concern had been purely in the interests of camp harmony. The rest was incidental.

'I think I'd rather go straight up, if you don't mind,' she said.

'Help yourself,' the other invited. 'You know where everything is.'

If she had been feeling any fatigue at all, it had dissipated by the time she was ready for bed. Rina had left a silk nightdress out for her. Cut to a deep V back and front, it fitted perfectly.

Lying in the darkness, she tried to compose herself for sleep, but sleep wouldn't come. She heard Rina come up some untold time later, heard the click of the other bedroom door. There came the distant sound of revelry from the direction of the town centre. The *cantinas* emptying, she surmised. In an hour or less, the KDC crew would be back on camp—apart from those who might have found somewhere else to spend the night. This time tomorrow she would be back there herself, and facing another week. If the prospect no longer held quite the same appeal, that was Brad's fault. He had done everything possible to ruin things for her. Last night had been pure calculation on his part all the way through. It wouldn't be happening again; she would make sure of that. If it took every ounce of grit and stamina she possessed, she would see this job through.

It was hopeless, she acknowledged after another half an hour had passed. She had seen some drinking chocolate in the kitchen. Perhaps if she went down and made herself a warm drink it would help.

The air was cool on her shoulders without a wrap, but not too uncomfortably so. The lightweight mules Rina had also left out were just a little bit too big and flapped as she walked. She took them off until she got downstairs so as not to waken her hostess, hastily donning them again when she saw something scuttle across the floor in the light of the lamp she lit.

In addition to the charcoal oven and grill, there was a small portable stove fuelled by Calor gas cylinders. Kerry made the chocolate with water, then added powdered milk. Not the best she'd ever tasted, she acknowledged, trying it, but good enough.

She took mug and lamp through to the living-room and curled up on a sofa to sip the drink. It was only just gone midnight, she realised in surprise, catching sight of the clock on the far wall. It seemed so much later. She could hear the distant sound of music still, so perhaps the crew hadn't yet left the town, after all. They would want to make the most of the one night of the week when they didn't have to consider an early start to the following morning.

The chocolate was doing the trick, she thought drowsily, putting the mug down on the low darkwood table. The sofa was so soft and comfortable, the rug she had pulled about her shoulders a more than adequate protection against the night air. Just a few minutes, she told herself, and then she would go back up to bed.

She awoke with a start when the outer door was opened. The lamplight flickered over Brad's face as he stood looking across at her, darkening his skin to a mahogany hue.

'Waiting for me?' he asked sardonically.

The rug had slipped from her shoulders. Kerry refrained with an effort from clutching it around her again, aware of the clinging brevity of the nightdress. He had held her nude in his arms last night, but that had been in total darkness.

'I thought you were supposed to be staying in Ciudad,' she said.

He came further into the room, sloughing his jacket as he moved. 'So I changed my mind.'

She wanted to get up and go, but he was too close for comfort. She felt desperately unsure of herself—even more so of him.

'Rina's in bed,' she said, and saw his mouth lift at the corner.

'So I gather. Why aren't you?'

'I couldn't sleep, so I came down to make myself a hot drink,' she explained, and knew her voice betrayed her. 'How did you get in?' she asked hurriedly.

'Rina never bothers locking the door,' he said. 'She trusts people.'

'Even you?'

Mockery infiltrated his regard. 'That's more like it. I was beginning to think I'd finally flattened you. Last night was——'

Heat flamed her cheeks. 'I don't want to talk about last night!'

'I was about to say last night was a mistake,' he continued inexorably. 'It should never have happened.'

Kerry gazed at him, the pain twisting inside her like a knife. 'It's a bit late to decide that, isn't it?' she managed at last. 'The damage is done.'

Some fleeting expression passed across the grey eyes. 'You could say that. I took the opportunity to phone your father while I was down there.'

'To tell him what?'

'That you'd arrived safely and were finding your feet.'

She was silent for a moment, hardly knowing how to react. 'Does that mean you're willing to accept me as a member of the team?'

'Not willing,' he said. 'Resigned.'

'Thanks.' Her tone was bitter. 'You certainly make sure of your pound of flesh first!'

He shrugged, his face registering little expression. 'We're not going to gain anything by going over the same ground. Just forget it.'

Forget it? she thought painfully. When every inch of her was crying out for him to touch her, to hold her, to take her again!

'You took a risk asking Rina to have me stay here tonight,' she said as he moved to the drinks cupboard. 'For all you know, I've told her everything.'

He had his back to her, hand reaching for the whisky bottle. 'I doubt it.'

'What makes you so sure?'

'Instinct. Something else there's no prerogative on.' The glass in his hand caught the soft light as he turned. 'I might have been forced to accept the situation, but the same difficulties still exist. You'll be staying here every Saturday night till the end of the contract.'

It took her a moment or two to find a response. 'Does Rina know?'

'Naturally. It was her suggestion.'

'Then you can tell her thanks, but no thanks. I've no intention of muscling in on your arrangement!'

'You won't be muscling in on any arrangement.' His voice had hardened. 'I rarely spend nights down here. In any case, you don't have a choice. I've already discussed it with Alan Pope first thing, and your father a few hours ago. They both saw the sense. On the face of it, I'd say your father is beginning to have some doubts about the wisdom of letting you come out here at all. He obviously didn't stop to think it through initially. Anyway, that's how it is. Take it or leave it. I have his full authority to send you packing if you start cutting up.'

Kerry gazed at him helplessly, her emotions in turmoil. She knew a sudden desperate urge to turn her back on the whole situation—except that to do so would be tantamount to acknowledging failure. This job was to pave the way to others of a similar nature. If she showed herself unable to cope with the pressures now, her father was hardly going to countenance any further experimentation.

'You take too much on yourself,' she said at last, fighting to keep her tone level. 'You had no right ringing Dad.'

'Somebody had to point out the problems.'

'Did you happen to mention that you were the biggest one?'

'Not any more.' He paused, eyeing her with a slant to his lips. 'It would be a lie to say you leave me cold. That nightdress is enough to turn a saint on! All the same, you're safe enough.'

'It's Rina's,' she said. 'I'd have thought you'd recognise it.' She got stiffly to her feet, too well aware of the translucency of the material in the glow of the lamplight. 'I'll leave you to savour your petty little triumphs!'

It took an effort to turn her back on him and move away—an even greater one to control the shakiness in her limbs. She wanted him so badly it was a physical pain deep inside her. Compared with that need, safety had no appeal whatsoever.

CHAPTER SEVEN

BREAKFAST was a trial. Served grilled ham and scrambled eggs, Kerry had to force herself to show some appreciation.

Seated opposite, Brad revealed no lack of appetite. Nor, if it came to that, did Rina herself. The latter looked like a woman who had just spent a satisfying night, Kerry thought hollowly. She hadn't heard Brad come upstairs, but then, with her head buried in the pillows to blot out that very sound, she wouldn't have, would she? They'd both of them been up and about before she had dragged herself out of bed.

The morning was fine, the temperature already into the low seventies. Glenn wouldn't be here until early afternoon, which left her with several hours to kill. What she was going to do with them she had no idea.

'I don't suppose there's a market on Sundays?' she asked tentatively over coffee.

It was Brad who answered, his voice cool. 'Even the peasants need a day off. If you're stuck for entertainment, you could always go to church.'

'I don't have anything to pray for,' she rejoined with saccharine sweetness. 'Perhaps I should go and wipe a few fevered brows up at the site. Judging from last night's racket, there's going to be no one in a fit state to even think about making a pass!'

'Some responses don't need thinking about.'

'I'm sure you'd know!' Catching Rina's glance, Kerry bit her lip. She was a guest in the other woman's home;

110

carrying on like this was no way to behave. 'I understand I'm supposed to be spending every Saturday night here,' she said on a calmer note. 'I'm very grateful for the offer, Rina, but I don't see any reason why you should have to be landed. If it's so essential for me to stay away from the site, I can always book into an hotel for the night.'

'I told you before, there isn't one suitable,' Brad put in before Rina could answer.

'I'm not proud.'

'Neither are the bugs.' His jaw was compressed. 'If you're trying to rile me, you're going the right way about it!'

'As a matter of interest,' Rina said mildly, 'when did you discuss it?'

'I was downstairs drinking hot chocolate when he arrived,' Kerry admitted with some diffidence. 'I hope you don't mind?'

The other's smile was faint. 'You're welcome. The same goes about staying here. A man with a skinful tends to revert to basic instincts—especially when he's had his appetite whetted by the local lights of love. I'm not saying they're all tarred with the same brush, but out of forty there's sure to be a few who can't tell one kind of woman from another. They're the ones you'd need to look out for.' Her eyes sought Brad's for a brief moment, their expression difficult to read, then came back. 'Have you decided what you're going to do about Miguel yet?'

Brad looked from one to the other of them enquiringly. 'What about Miguel?'

'He's demanding payment for the car Kerry hired,' supplied Rina when the former failed to answer. 'With menaces, according to what Glenn said.'

Some expression came and went in the grey eyes. 'Ingram was here?'

'He drove me down from the site,' Kerry acknowledged. 'Rina invited him to supper.'

'And he went with you to see Miguel?'

'Yes.' She met his gaze squarely. 'He tried reasoning with him, but Miguel wouldn't have it. He wants the money by Monday, which was when I was due to return the car, or he's going to inform the police.'

'Do you think there's any danger of him making a case?' asked Rina.

Broad shoulders lifted. 'Depends how well in he is with the local cops. If there's money involved, they'll probably be more than ready to back him. How much is he asking for?'

'It works out at around eight hundred pounds,' Kerry admitted wryly. 'I suppose that's a small enough price to stay out of gaol—although I'm going to have to ask for some extra time to get it wired through from home.'

Brad's smile was dry. 'Miguel never owned any car worth more than a hundred, and that's erring on the generous side!' He glanced at his watch, pushed back his chair. 'Come on.'

Kerry didn't move. 'I told you, Glenn already tried to talk him out of it.'

'Constant dripping wears away stone,' he said. 'Let's go.'

She obeyed because there didn't seem to be any choice. Rina shook her head when invited to accompany them.

'I can't stand bloodshed,' she said humorously. 'See you when you get back.'

A Land Rover was parked out on the street. Kerry balked at the idea of using it. 'The garage is only just down the hill,' she said. 'We could walk.'

'Miguel won't be there at this time,' Brad returned. 'I've a good idea where he lives. We'll beard the old fox in his den.'

'Foxes live in earths,' she said pedantically, and caught his impatient glance.

'Do you want help or don't you?'

'Yes,' she admitted with reluctance.

'Then get in the car.'

The Mexican had a house in one of the better areas on the far side of the town. Several children were at play in the colourful courtyard, and one of them ran obligingly to fetch his father in answer to Brad's request.

Miguel looked more than a little disconcerted to see Kerry, though his recovery was swift. Brad wasted no time in broaching the subject, only to receive the same answer given the previous day.

'I told you it wouldn't be any use,' Kerry murmured resignedly.

He shut her up with a warning glance. 'Supposing you go and wait in the car,' he said.

Futile, she thought, but she went. When he joined her barely two minutes later he offered no comment, simply turning the vehicle around and heading back the way they had come.

'Thanks for trying, anyway,' she said after a moment or two. 'Did he agree to wait for his money?'

'He's decided to write the car off as a gesture of goodwill,' Brad replied levelly.

She studied the strong profile in confusion. 'I don't understand. What made him change his mind so suddenly?'

'I told him I'd bring a gang down and smash up his garage if he pursued the same line.'

Green eyes darkened. 'I see. Bully-boy tactics!'

'They're the only ones his kind understands.' He shot her a glance, lips thinning. 'You'd as soon have forked out the eight hundred?'

'If it came to a choice between that and this, yes!'

'So offer what *you* think the car was worth. He'll snatch your hand off and think you're a fool.'

'Better a fool than a mobster!' she retorted with heat. 'I didn't ask you to interfere.'

'True.' The anger was threatening to boil over. 'Of all the mule-headed females I ever met, you just about take the prize! Maybe I should take you back there and let you sort it out for yourself!'

Teeth gritted, she said, 'There wouldn't have been any problem in the first place if Pete Lomas hadn't pushed the car off the road!'

'So try asking him for a contribution.' He slammed the Land Rover round a corner, narrowly missing a mangy-looking cat about to set off across the road. 'I'm sure he'll be ready to oblige.'

She had no answer ready for that one. Most of her sniping stemmed directly from last night's emotional frustration, she admitted ruefully. He probably knew it, too.

They were almost back to Rina's before she could bring herself to make some move towards reconciliation.

'I realise I should be grateful,' she offered on a diffident note. 'It's just that I——'

'It's just that you'd as soon not be under any obligation to me,' he finished for her. 'Consider it a fair return for services already rendered.'

The shaft found its mark, as it was meant to do. Kerry turned her head away and stared out of the window, blinking furiously at the moisture gathering at the corners of her eyes. She had asked for it, she supposed, but it didn't make it any easier to bear. The only feeling Brad had for her was contempt.

Rina had coffee waiting for them. She accepted the assurance that matters had been sorted out without asking any further detail. Kerry made an excuse to escape to her bedroom after a while. She felt too choked up to stay in company with the two of them. With Rina, Brad was a different man. They were easy together—almost like husband and wife. Even if the American woman did learn he had made love to her, she had a feeling she would take it in her stride. If this was to be the pattern of the weekends, she thought disconsolately, then Brad might even get his own way in the end.

Glenn arrived at three as arranged to pick her up. His manner seemed odd, Kerry thought, greeting him at the car.

'I see Brad got back,' he said, indicating the other vehicle.

'He came back last night,' she confirmed. 'Any trouble on camp last night?'

'A couple of fist fights—nothing out of the way.' There was still that same constriction in his voice. 'Where would you like to go?'

'You were going to show me the rest of the town,' she reminded him.

'Oh, yes.' He sounded about as enthusiastic as she felt. 'Not that there's so much more of it to see.'

The afternoon could scarcely be called a resounding success. It was Kerry herself who finally suggested they call it a day and find somewhere to eat.

Seated in one of the better-class restaurants just re-opened after siesta, she took the bull by the horns. 'You're all on edge, Glenn. Is there something wrong?'

He looked uncomfortable, eyes not quite meeting hers. 'I'm not sure how to say it.'

'How about straight out?' she invited.

'All right.' He still didn't look at her directly. 'There's a rumour going round that you spent the night with Brad Halston on Friday.'

Pete Lomas was the only possible source, she thought numbly. 'And you believed it, of course,' she said on an unemotional note.

This time he did look at her, his face troubled. 'It doesn't matter what I believe, it's what you're going to be up against when you get back up there.'

She forced a shrug. 'I suppose it was odds on it was going to happen. *En masse*, men are just as bad as women for spreading malicious gossip.'

'Then it isn't true?'

'No.' Strictly speaking, it was no lie, she reflected.

Relief lit his features, followed swiftly by discomfiture. 'I should have known. I'm sorry, Kerry. It was just that you and he . . . well, there's always an undercurrent between you. It seemed——

'It's all right.' It wasn't, and probably never would be, but it was all she could say. 'The fact of the matter is that Pete Lomas followed me from the rec. on Friday night, and Brad happened to see him.'

'You mean Lomas tried to jump you?'

'In a word, yes. He's the only one who could have started the rumour. Everybody else was tied up by the storm.'

'Then he should be faced with it!'

'It wouldn't do any good,' she returned wryly. 'Denials only make things worse. The only way is to turn a deaf ear. Rumours need fuel to keep them alive.'

'Shouldn't you at least warn Brad what to expect?'

There was no way she was going back to Rina's place again today, Kerry told herself. She didn't even want to think about the two of them alone together.

'He'll find out soon enough,' she said. 'What was the road like coming down?'

'Clear enough not to cause any problems. All the same,' he added, 'it might be a good idea if we made it back before dark. You just never know when there's going to be another rockfall.'

'Did KDC run the road through?' she asked, eager for something—anything—to take her mind off the former subject.

'They just widened it to take heavier traffic,' he said. 'It goes right on up into the mountains.'

'You've been up past the dam yourself?'

'A couple of times. It's navigable for four-wheel drive. There's some ruins up there. Looks like there used to be a village or something. They can't be of any archaeological interest. From what I could tell, nobody's been near the place in years. I could take you up one weekend, if you like?'

'That might be an idea,' she agreed lightly. 'It sounds interesting.'

The daily downpour had come and gone by the time they were ready to leave. Glenn had left the Land Rover parked on a side-street. It had been running fine when they had arrived, but when he came to turn on the ignition there wasn't even a spark.

'Can't understand it,' he said, perplexed, taking a look under the bonnet. 'Not that engines are really my thing. I'm going to have to get help.'

'Not from Miguel, I hope?' Kerry asked.

'Only as a last resort. There's a mechanic of sorts has a yard not too far from here. He'd be the best bet, if I can get hold of him.' He closed the bonnet down again with a resigned expression. 'Look, this could take hours. It might be best if you went back to Rina's place. I can always pick you up again once I'm mobile.'

There was really no other way, Kerry acknowledged hollowly. She could hardly sit here for hours on end.

'I'll see you back there first,' he said as she climbed reluctantly from the vehicle. 'Pete Lomas was on the truck that came down earlier. After what you told me, he's the last person you'll want to run into on your own.'

It took them about ten minutes to make the journey on foot. With nightfall not so very far away, the townsfolk were beginning to appear on the streets, the younger element to promenade, the more mature to sit and drink and talk and generally enjoy the Sunday evening ritual. Dressed as she was in trousers and shirt, Kerry felt the cynosure of all eyes. She was relieved when they reached the comparative solitude of the street where Rina's house was situated.

Glenn took her as far as the courtyard entrance. 'Not much point in my coming in with you,' he said. 'Best if I get straight on to finding Enrique. Hopefully that won't take too long.' He hesitated a moment. 'Perhaps you should go up with Brad.'

'Always providing he isn't planning on staying the night,' she came back evenly. 'Good luck, anyway.'

'Thanks,' he said. 'I'll need it.'

She watched him down the hill before making a move towards the house. 'Sorry,' she proffered ruefully when Rina opened the door to her knock. 'We had a breakdown. Glenn's trying to find a mechanic.'

It was difficult, as always, to tell what the American woman's true thoughts were. 'Don't stand on ceremony,' she said. 'Come on in.'

Brad was on his feet, his expression equally un-revealing. He had on the denim jacket he had been wearing on his arrival the previous night.

'So what went wrong?' he asked.

'The engine wouldn't start,' she said. 'We left it parked while we had a meal. Do you think there's any possibility that Miguel had something to do with it? I mean, if he happened to be passing and recognised the KDC markings.'

His smile was derisive. 'An ordinary breakdown not dramatic enough for you?'

She bit down hard on the retort that rose to her lips. 'Just a thought, that's all.'

'Lucky you got here when you did,' said Rina. 'Brad was just about to leave.'

Kerry said swiftly, 'Glenn is going to call for me when he gets the car fixed.'

'There's every likelihood that won't be before morning, so you'd better come back with me.' Brad ran an eye over her, his mouth taking on an added slant. 'Don't you have a jacket? It's going to be dark before we get there.'

'I left it in the Land Rover,' she confessed, only now remembering.

'I've a poncho you can use,' offered Rina. 'You can always return it next weekend.' She was moving as she spoke. 'It's in my room. I'll get it for you.'

The silence when she'd gone could almost be felt. Kerry was the first to break it. 'There's something you should know before we get back on site.'

Dark brows lifted. 'And what's that?'

Rina's reappearance with the poncho cut short her reply. She slid the garment over her head with a word of thanks, wishing she could find something to dislike about the older woman. Brad didn't deserve her, and that was a fact!

The leavetaking was casual enough, but then they had had all afternoon to be otherwise. Brad waited until he had the car in motion before saying levelly, 'So what is it I should know?'

It took her a moment to find the words. 'It seems to be the general opinion that we spent Friday night together.'

The pause was lengthy. When he did speak it was with no change of inflection. 'Is that it?'

Kerry shot him a glance, hardly able to believe he could be taking it so calmly. 'Isn't it enough?'

He shrugged. 'It had to come sooner or later. If it hadn't been me, you'd have been linked with somebody else. Lomas, if he'd had his way—or even Glenn Ingram. You've certainly spent enough time with him.'

'I work with him. Of course we spend time together!'

'I'm not talking about work. Lucky I was the one nominated.'

'Lucky?'

'That's right. Not even Lomas is going to jeopardise his job by trying to muscle in on territory I'm already credited with laying claim to.'

'There's no credit attached,' she retorted bitingly. 'Even if it were true——'

'It is true. Mostly, at any rate. Try denying it, and you'll simply add fuel to the fire.'

She lifted a hand in a helpless little gesture. 'So how *do* we tackle it?'

'Quite simply, we don't.'

'I can't allow people like Alan Pope to think I'm sleeping with you!'

'He's a man himself,' came the dry retort. 'What's to say he hasn't entertained a few of the same notions where you're concerned this last week?'

'He isn't like that!'

'This side of eighty, we're *all* like that. Some are better at concealing it than others, that's all. It's a natural instinct.'

'Not in my book!'

'To underline the obvious, you're not a man. Which brings us right back to square one.'

'I'm not going to be driven out.' Her voice was low. 'Not by you or anybody!'

'Then you're going to have to put up with whatever comes your way.' He sounded close to the edge of tolerance. 'This fiancé of yours must be a pretty easygoing guy.'

Kerry stiffened. 'Who told you about Tim?'

'Who do you think? You were ready enough to let Rina in on the secret.' They were heading up the first steep incline, the deep shadows cast by the setting sun stretching out to envelop them. 'It wasn't him you were thinking about the other night, for sure,' he added softly.

'I don't recall being giving the chance to say no,' she forced out.

'You didn't want it.'

That was too near the truth for comfort. She said tautly, 'I dare say you could make any woman respond if you put your mind to it. You've had enough experience.'

'No more than any other man my age.' He paused, and his tone subtly altered as he said, 'How old is this Tim?'

'Twenty-nine.' The words were dragged from her. 'He helped design this very dam.'

'Bully for him. Is he as good in the sack?'

She drew in a heavy breath. 'That doesn't even merit an answer!'

'From which I gather it's either no, or I don't know. If it's the first he's no use to you, if the second then he most likely won't be. Either way——'

She kicked out suddenly and viciously at the ankle nearest to her, too incensed to heed the danger. The Land Rover swerved towards the edge of the drop, was brought back sharply under control, and then to an abrupt stop under the lee of the mountainside.

'You damned little fool!' Brad gritted. 'You could have had us over!'

She was white-faced herself, but the anger overrode all. 'Tim's worth three of you!' she spat at him. 'Any day of the week!'

His eyes sparked. 'If he was anything of a man he'd have put his foot down about your coming out here in the first place!'

She said cuttingly, 'You wouldn't understand the kind of relationship we share. Tim regards me as an individual, not an appendage. He respects my right to make my own choices.'

'Like your father before him. Or is it that it's simply less trouble for them both to let you go your own way?'

There was a hard obstruction in her throat, making speech difficult. 'Are you accusing Dad of not caring?'

'I'm suggesting,' he said hardily, 'that his judgement could be improved on.'

'Supposing you stick to sorting out your own relationships.'

He gave her a narrow smile. 'I wasn't aware I had one to sort.'

'Meaning you'll be leaving Rina flat once this contract is finished, I suppose?'

'Hardly flat,' he responded. 'She doesn't have the shape for it.' The shrug was brief. 'She'll be going back to California. I'm not sure yet what my plans are. Does that answer the question?'

Kerry was unable to hold his gaze. 'It's going to be dark in a few minutes,' she said. 'Shouldn't we be going?'

'Scared I might be considering a repeat performance?' His mouth was cruel as he shook his head. 'You can rest easy. I shan't be touching you again. I need my head examined for doing it at all!'

Darkness descended with its customary swiftness once the sun was gone. Brad drove with caution, headlights cutting a wide swathe ahead. The minor rockfalls they had met the previous day had been joined by others of a slightly more serious nature. Another job for the bulldozer in the morning, Kerry assumed.

Judging by the lights in the recreation room when they finally reached the site, some of the men were already back. Either that, or they hadn't bothered going into town again after last night's excesses. She was glad to find the senior personnel hut apparently empty of residents. Tomorrow would be soon enough to face the speculation.

'Thanks for the lift,' she said when Brad paused at his room door. 'I'll try to stay out of your way.'

He made no reply to that. She didn't suppose there was anything much *to* say. He had made himself clear enough. No further interest.

She heard him go out again some little time later. No skulking in the cabin for Brad Halston. He would look the rumour-mongers in the eye without a flicker. It would probably be better if she went and did the same, but she lacked the courage. Things always seemed less important by daylight, she reassured herself, and wished she could believe it.

The night was long, and far from restful. She got up bleary-eyed and depressed. Because of the necessity of waiting until everyone else had cleared the ablutions, she was always late in to breakfast. This morning she gave it a miss altogether, setting out to walk to the site office. She could only hope that Glenn had managed to get back. Right now he seemed her only ally.

The sound of a bulldozer rumbling up in her wake stiffened muscle and sinew. She stepped to one side to let it pass, looking up into Pete Lomas's sneering face without expression as he brought the vehicle down to idling pace.

'No chauffeur service?' he jeered. 'What happened to lover-boy, then?'

'I've no idea what you're talking about,' she said.

'The hell you haven't!' He spat contemptuously. 'Women like you make me puke!'

'Strange.' Kerry kept her voice under strict control. 'Men like you affect me in exactly the same way. Do carry on, Mr Lomas. I prefer my air unpolluted.'

'You'll get yours,' he threatened. 'You and Halston both! Nobody makes a fool of me!'

'They don't need to,' she retorted scathingly, abandoning her stance. 'You make an excellent job of it yourself!'

He mouthed a few choice obscenities at her, then slammed the engine back into gear. Kerry waited until the machine was well ahead before making any move to follow. She was trembling a little, uncomfortably aware that disdainful silence would have been a more effective weapon against his type. All the same, she doubted if his threats meant anything. As Brad had said, he wouldn't risk his job with KDC.

Finding Glenn already present when she reached the site office was a relief. He had managed to get the Land Rover fixed within the hour, it appeared, so he couldn't have been all that far behind them.

'Seems the rotor arm had somehow gone missing,' he said when Kerry asked what had been wrong with the vehicle. 'Not something you'd even notice without taking the distributor cap off,' he added, as if in self-defence. 'Lucky Enrique was able to find a spare. Must have been some kids playing around for laughs.'

That made rather more sense than her former suspicion, Kerry was bound to concede. Aware of the covert glances directed her way from the other side of the glass partition, she said softly, 'I gather rumour is still rife?'

'You did say to leave well alone,' he reminded her.

'I know. I just don't have what it takes to ignore the whole thing.'

'It's either that, or stand up and deny it.' Glenn paused. 'Does Brad know?'

'I told him last night,' she confirmed. 'Not that it seemed to bother him at all. Different for a man, though, isn't it? Just another feather in his cap!' She caught herself up, meeting the hazel eyes with a faint smile. 'You're the exception rather than the rule, Glenn.'

His own smile was wry. 'Depends what we're talking about. Perhaps the day will come when we'll all be able to accept women on site as an everyday occurrence, but it isn't going to happen overnight. You've been the main topic of conversation since you got here. I suppose you'll go on being it until——'

'Until I pack my bags and get back where I belong?'

'I was going to say until the job's finished.'

Kerry sighed. 'Sorry, I jumped the gun. Would you say I'm resented?'

'By some, perhaps, not all.' He made an incisive movement. 'I have to get the monthly financial statement and report ready for dispatch. Want to sit in?'

He was right, she thought. The job had to come ahead of everything else. 'Love to,' she said.

Apart from fleeting glimpses in the canteen at lunchtime, she saw nothing of Brad all day. Going in there, the focus of all eyes for several unnerving seconds, was the most difficult thing she had ever done. She was grateful to Glenn for keeping a conversation going.

Alan Pope had made no comment, but it was obvious that he too had heard the rumour. Whether he believed it or not was immaterial, Kerry supposed. The damage lay in the very fact of its existence. Should it be discovered that she was to spend every weekend at the home of Brad's lady-friend, the fat would really be in the fire. It would most likely be assumed he was running a *ménage à trois*!

Playing gooseberry was almost as bad, she reflected, and came to a firm decision. Better to take her chances up here than to suffer that ignominy. She could always barricade her door again.

The situation gradually began to assume less importance as the week progressed. One could, Kerry reckoned with a certain cynicism, learn to take anything in one's stride, given time. She made no particular effort to avoid Brad, though he seemed to be steering clear of her. On the one or two occasions when they did happen to meet face to face, there was no exchange beyond the casual greeting suited to the time of day. He had even discarded the mockery, she noted. When he looked at her now it was with total detachment.

By Friday she had made her plans. Not even Glenn was to be privy to them. This was something she had to do on her own. Once Brad got the message that she wasn't going to be pushed around, he might stop trying to organise her life. She was quite capable of looking out for her own interests.

'Would there be any objection to my using the spare Rover over the weekend?' she asked Alan casually before leaving the office that evening. 'I'd like to be independent for transport.'

He gave her a quizzical glance. 'Afraid of giving Glenn the wrong idea? Better if you didn't pay him too much attention, agreed. I might stand a chance of getting his mind back wholly on his work again.'

Kerry made a small, wry gesture. 'I take it that means I can have the Land Rover?'

'Seems like it. Just take care, will you? I dread having to give your father bad news.'

Telling Glenn she wouldn't be driving down to Las Meridas with him the following afternoon wasn't easy. He didn't even try to conceal his feelings.

'I thought you trusted me,' he said gruffly.

'I do,' she assured him. 'I just need some time to myself, that's all.'

'You're hardly going to get that at Rina's.' He paused, then went on in an altered tone, 'Unless it's Brad you're really going to meet.'

She said with emphasis, 'Rina is the only woman he's interested in. He arranged for me to stay there simply to save his precious men from having to fight their male instincts when they get back from town boozed up to the eyes—there was no other reason.'

Glenn sighed. 'It makes sense, I suppose. As project manager, he's responsible for anything and everything that happens on site. Not that we couldn't provide adequate protection ourselves, if it came to that.'

'I don't want anyone keeping guard outside my door,' she retorted firmly. 'If I'm going to do this job at all I have to be able to stand on my own feet.' She caught herself up before she said any more. 'I'd better be going, or I'll still be in the shower when the hooter blows. See you later, Glenn.'

With the Land Rover at her disposal, she was back at the compound in a few minutes. Judging by the smells issuing forth from the kitchen shack, dinner was already well under way.

The rain had come early today, the residue still standing around in puddles of mud. The surrounding mountain-tops were outlined against a sky washed clean. Looking back beyond the dam, Kerry remembered what Glenn had said about the village ruins. They alone would make the trip worthwhile. If she left while everybody was milling around preparing for the exodus into town tomorrow, it was doubtful if her departure would be noticed. If Brad checked up on her at all he would assume she was already on her way down to Las Meridas. By the time it was finally realised she wasn't going to show up at Rina's place for the night, she would be safely ensconced in her own room here with a pile of magazines from the recreation room for entertainment.

Not the ideal way to spend a Saturday evening, she was bound to admit, but better than allowing herself to be governed by Brad's dictate. What she was going to do on subsequent weekends she hadn't yet considered. If she was honest with herself, she was beginning to doubt her ability to last out till the end of the contract, although the thought of giving in was unpalatable. Brad's fault, mostly. In future she would make sure to avoid any job in which KDC were involved.

She refused to acknowledge the bleakness that any future in which Brad didn't figure engendered. Her career meant more to her overall than any man!

Fresh from her shower, and clad in the white boiler-suit she used solely for the purpose of crossing the compound, she was hanging out some items of underwear on the line she had rigged when the tap came on the door.

Joe, the cook, made a habit of sending his helpmate across with a mug of hot tea and a sandwich for her around this time. A blunt Yorkshireman, with a heart of pure gold, he thought her undernourished and in need of cosseting. Smiling at the thought, Kerry went to open the door, the word of thanks fading on her lips when she saw Brad standing there.

'Taking an early bath?' she asked, making a swift recovery. 'One of the perks of being boss man, I suppose!'

'One of them,' he agreed imperturbably. 'Not, as it happens, what I'm here for.'

She kept a firm hold on the door, as much to counteract the weakness in her knees as to keep him from entering the room. 'So what *are* you here for?'

'To make sure you hadn't forgotten our arrangements for tomorrow night,' he said.

'*Your* arrangements,' she corrected coolly. 'I'd hardly forget a thing like that, would I?'

The grey eyes revealed little. 'Who knows? Be ready for half-past one.'

'And have it look as if we're spending the whole weekend together?' She was hard put to it to keep her tone even. 'I've arranged my own transport, thanks.'

His gaze narrowed. 'With Ingram?'

'No, not with Glenn. Alan allowed me use of the spare Rover.'

'Strictly speaking, all site transport is under KDC authority, but I dare say the point can be stretched. Just don't go smashing it up.'

Kerry bit back the hasty retort. There was nothing to be gained from a slanging match. 'I'll try my best,' she promised ambiguously. 'Would you tell Rina I'll be eating out? I don't want to put her to any more trouble than I have to.'

His nod suggested indifference. 'Your choice. Just be there.'

Not for a million dollars, she thought, feeling the ache in her chest deepen as he turned to go. To see him and Rina together again would be more than she could bear.

CHAPTER EIGHT

GETTING off site the following afternoon proved no problem at all. Kerry was pretty sure that if anyone had noted the Land Rover heading back towards the dam they would have assumed it was being driven by one of the skeleton crew left to guard the place against possible interlopers.

Once cut off from view of the valley floor by the buttresses of rock, she eased up on the accelerator. It needed five hours or more until nightfall. Plenty of time to make the village Glenn had told her about, and get back.

She brought the vehicle to a stop at the dam head in order to view the terrain she was to cover. Seen from up here, the landscape had a wild, uncharted look, bringing a momentary doubt, swiftly swamped by determination. Glenn had been there before her. What he could do so could she! Wasn't it her very ability to hold her own in this so-called man's world that she was out to prove?

The dam itself drew her like a magnet. With Alan's ban still in force, this might be the only chance she would have of overcoming her weakness. It was her head, after all.

She got out of the Land Rover with purpose, steeling her nerves against the slight tremor in her limbs. All she had to do was walk a little way out and stand there for a few minutes while her balance adjusted. She wouldn't go near the edge.

Thinking it was one thing, doing it another. Only by exerting all her will-power could she make her legs carry her forward on to the curving surface. Comparatively narrow though the gorge was, the opposite side looked to be a mile away from this angle. Kerry came to a halt some twenty or so feet out to draw in steadying breaths of the clear mountain air. Five full minutes, she told herself. Just five minutes, and then retreat. Surely she could manage that?

Gazing at the sweeping panorama, she felt her stomach muscles begin to loosen up a little. Hardly an immediate cure, but it did prove that the only way she was going to get round the problem was by facing up to it. If Alan could only be convinced of it, too, she could have the thing conquered.

There was a lot of activity over on the camp site as the waiting trucks started to fill. It gave her a certain feeling of superiority to be looking at the scene from such a height. The realisation that if she could see them they could also see her sent her scuttling back to the security of the rock cover at a pace she would have considered breakneck bare minutes ago. Not that they'd any of them be taking an interest in the dam wall at a time like this, she reflected, gaining the car again. Wine, women and song were the order of the day!

As Glenn had warned her, the track beyond the dam was rough. What he hadn't said was that having once taken it, turning a vehicle round was virtually impossible. At least it settled the question of whether or not she continued with this jaunt of hers.

Pine trees crowded the slopes both above and below, clearing here and there to afford superb views of the surrounding peaks. At one point the road skirted a fast-flowing stream which she took to be one of the tributaries that would feed the dam. From the amount of water coming down, there had been recent rain higher up in the mountains. To be caught up here in a storm of the other night's proportions would be no joke, she acknowledged soberly. Right now the sky was clear, but that didn't mean it couldn't cloud over. With the rainy season proper just getting into its stride, there was no predicting what might happen.

Obviously she had to be able to turn the Land Rover round when she reached this village, she comforted herself. Otherwise Glenn would never have made it back. She'd been a fool to attempt this on her own. She had to admit that now. Not that knowing it helped her predicament.

There was still no sign of the village when she reached the uppermost edge of the tree line, just the track clinging to the side of the mountain. Rounding a bend to see the jumble of earth and rock spilled halfway across was a heart-jerking shock. With still no room to turn, she had no choice but to edge the Land Rover past with its wheels on the very rim of the drop, pausing at the other side to wipe the beads of perspiration from her upper lip. So much for vertigo! After this, walking the dam top would be a doddle.

From there the whole thing became a nightmare. At times the track itself seemed to fade out, leaving her to pick a route as best she could. At one point she heard a deep rumbling sound coming from somewhere back along the way she had come. It lasted several seconds, and left a fear she didn't care to examine too closely. Reaching this village at all was her present priority.

It was almost six when she finally achieved that aim. With the best will in the world, she couldn't hope to get back to the dam again before dark, she thought numbly, bringing the Land Rover to a stop to sit gazing at the tumbled ruins. The view to the west across range after range was magnificent, though scarcely adequate compensation for her plight. Unless she was prepared to risk being caught halfway down that track when darkness fell, she was stuck here till morning without food or heat, or even a torch to see by.

She climbed stiffly from the car to investigate her surroundings, aware of her solitude as she had never been aware before. So far as she could tell, she was standing in the centre of what had once been a small plaza surrounded by buildings. Most of the latter were little more than a heap of rubble, but here and there a wall stood proud. It was odd, even eerie, to think that people had once lived here—that children had played in this square, heaven only knew how long ago. An isolated community, whatever. Las Meridas had to be at least two days' journey by *burro* from here.

None of which was of any great importance just now. Mexico had wildlife other than birds, and though the chances of coming face to face with a puma might be fairly remote, they did inhabit the mountain areas. Reptiles, too, if it came to that. With the sun already disappearing behind the higher peaks, the temperature was dropping by the minute. The Land Rover itself was her only refuge.

She'd been an utter fool, Kerry acknowledged bleakly. She'd set out on this trip with but one thought in mind, and that was to prove something to Brad. All she had proved was her lack of responsibility. With any luck, she would make it back to camp tomorrow before he took it into his head to come looking for her. His scorn if he knew the extent of her folly would be past all endurance.

In the meantime she could at least look for water while she could still see. Thirst was already becoming a problem.

She headed for the rear of the settlement, picking her way carefully around and between the ruins. Once, she saw something glide away from under a dislodged stone to vanish into the scant undergrowth, and wished she were wearing her boots. The various rustlings she put down largely to the breeze which had sprung up. Allowing her imagination to run away with her could only lead to panic. If nothing else, she had to keep a level head.

She heard the water before she saw it. Bubbling from a rocky outcropping, the spring fell into a small pool gouged out by primitive tools. It looked clear enough; she could only trust to luck that it was free of any parasites.

With nothing available in which to carry a supply, she had to content herself with drinking her fill. Quenching her thirst served to underline her hunger, but there was nothing she could do about that.

By the time she got back to the Land Rover the light was almost gone. It was going to be a long, long night, she thought miserably, huddling into a corner of the seat. At least she had had the sense to sling her denim jacket in the back. It afforded her some slight comfort.

She felt safer with the doors locked. Broken only by the occasional faint cry of some animal or other, the silence out there was almost tangible. Eventually she dozed off, awakening with a jerk some unknown time later to the rattling of the door-handle as something outside pawed at it.

Terror robbed her of all ability to move or shout. Eyes fixed, heart thudding into her throat, she waited for whatever it was out there to break down the door and leap at her. If she was going to die let it be quick, she prayed desperately.

The sight of the face at the window brought a low moan to her lips. It took whole seconds for the sound of Brad's voice to penetrate the frozen waste that was her mind. Sobbing with relief, she flung herself across the vehicle to take off the lock, too far gone to care about anything other than the fact that he was there.

Then he was in the Land Rover with her, his warmth and hardness a haven she never wanted to leave again.

'How did you find me?' she managed to ask when the trembling had lessened somewhat. 'How did you know where I'd gone?'

'I was on the point of leaving when I spotted you up on the dam wall,' he said. 'I probably wouldn't have realised it was you if you'd been wearing your hat.'

'It was a spur-of-the-moment thing,' Kerry admitted, her face still buried in his shirt-front. 'I wanted to prove I could do it, even if only for my own benefit. I didn't go near the edge.'

'Hardly a justification.' There was no softness in his voice. 'Does common sense come into anything you do?'

'Doesn't seem like it.' Her own voice was muffled. 'Don't go on at me, Brad.'

'Go on at you?' His laugh was entirely devoid of humour. 'For two pins——' He broke off, clamping his jaw. 'What in hell's name did you think you were doing setting off up here on your own? This is Mexico, not the damned Lake District!'

'I know.' She forced herself to sit up straight and meet his eyes. 'It was stupid of me, I realise that now. I thought the village was fairly close. Glenn said——'

'Don't try laying the blame at his door. Driving even half a kilometre into this kind of country without either map or equipment is idiotic—and that's putting it mildly!

I couldn't believe it when I got up there to the dam head and saw your tyre tracks heading out!'

His anger was justified, Kerry supposed, but it wasn't helping matters. 'Can we leave the recriminations till later?' she said, low-toned. 'I could sit here apologising all night and it wouldn't change anything. Is there any chance at all of getting back down that track before daylight?'

'There's no chance of getting down that track in any light,' he stated grimly. 'The whole damned mountainside fell on it a couple of kilometres back. You must have heard the noise.'

She stared at him in numb realisation. 'You mean both vehicles are stuck up here?'

'One vehicle. Mine's buried under a ton of rubble. Lucky I heard it coming and managed to get clear in time. It's taken me three hours to find a way round on foot. Even then, it was sheer luck that I finished up on the right heading.'

'Oh, God!' Her throat was so dry she could scarcely get the words out. 'You could have been killed, Brad!'

'But obviously wasn't.' His voice had lost none of its hardness. 'We can't do anything until morning, so we may as well try and get some sleep.'

She swallowed thickly. 'What's Rina going to think?'

'I've no idea,' he said. 'If I'd realised what your plans were I'd have made sure somebody knew about it. As it is, we're on our own. First time we're likely to be missed is Monday morning.'

Kerry searched the strong features outlined against the paler square of the window. 'You mean there's a possibility we might not make it back before then?'

He took a moment to answer that one. 'We've roughly fifteen kilometres to cover. In this kind of country we'll be lucky to average one an hour. If we set off at first light, we might just stand a chance before dark.'

'I don't understand,' she said in confusion. 'You made it up here in three hours from the landslide, and most of that in darkness. Surely we can go down the same way, then follow the track?'

Brad shook his head. 'That whole side is unstable. Our best bet will be to follow a watercourse. From what I remember of the topographical map, the stream that starts up here runs into the main course just above the dam gorge. If we can get that far, we should be able to work our way round.'

Kerry sagged back into the corner of her seat again, only now beginning to appreciate the full import of their situation. 'I've made a real mess of things, haven't I?' she said miserably.

Brad made no attempt to dispute the point. 'We'll be better off in the back,' he said. 'Just sit tight while I sort it out.'

The draught of cool night air inwards when he opened the rear made her thankful for the shelter. What she would have done if he hadn't spotted her on the dam and followed her, she hated to think. She wouldn't have stood a chance of finding her own way back.

'Will the vehicles be covered by insurance?' she asked hesitantly, wondering what her father would have to say if presented with a bill for two Land Rovers.

'Should be,' he said.

'I suppose it might even be possible to get this one lifted out by helicopter?' she hazarded, with memories of various war films she had seen.

'It would take a Sikorsky. Hiring one of those would cost more than a replacement, even if there was one available.' Brad finished letting down the rear seats, then got in and pulled the rear closed again. Crouching, he added, 'Not exactly the Ritz, but beggars can't be choosers. Come on through and try it out for space.'

Kerry slid between the two front seats with some reluctance, very much aware of his closeness. She let herself down on her side with her back to him, holding her breath as he eased himself down behind her. An arm came about her waist to pull her up firmly against him, his knees tucking themselves under the crook of hers. She could feel his breath stirring the hair at her nape, the beat of his heart in the region of her shoulder-blade.

'Relax,' he murmured close by her ear. 'We're going to need the body heat.'

If anything, her body was overheating, she thought desperately as the moments passed. She wanted to turn towards him, to feel his lips on hers. The fact that he had no feeling for her beyond a certain physical attraction had little bearing right now—although it would matter again tomorrow.

'You're not making this any easier,' he growled softly.

'I can't help it,' she whispered. 'Brad, I——'

'Just go to sleep.' He sounded weary. 'It's going to be a long, hard day.'

She did sleep eventually, but not deeply enough to drown out the storm which erupted around midnight. Compared with this, the other night was as nothing. Up here it felt as if every flash of lightning, every crashing explosion was aimed directly at their flimsy shelter. The rain sounded like machine-gun bullets on the metal roof.

'We're safe enough,' Brad assured her, awake too, and obviously aware of her fear. 'The tyres would earth any strike. It always sounds worse in the mountains because of the echoes.'

Almost as if in direct response came a flash of lightning that lit the car like daylight, followed immediately by a clap of thunder which jerked her upright like a puppet pulled by strings.

Shaking, she was dimly aware of Brad hauling himself to a sitting position beside her. Then his arms were around her again, pulling her across him to hold her close against his chest. She clung to him in an intensity of emotion in which terror played only a part, turning her face up beseechingly, her lips begging the comfort he was withholding from her.

The muscles tautened in his jaw as he bent his head towards her. That first seeking, demanding pressure offered no soft options. He wanted her the way she wanted him. Hard and unyielding as the floor of the Land Rover was, she didn't feel it. The touch of Brad's hands, his lips, his masculine scent, those were the only things she was conscious of.

Kneeling over her, he removed his jacket and folded it into a pillow for her head—a gesture which melted what little resistance might still have lingered in her heart. She was ready, even eager, to assist him in taking off her clothing, not even conscious of the chill when she lay naked under his eyes, nor minding the lightning which revealed her to him in such intimate detail. There was nothing she wouldn't do for this man, she thought mistily—no problems she couldn't surmount. Rina had faded into the background—a shadowy figure no longer of any importance.

The feel of his hands and lips on her body was ecstasy. She tore at his shirt, pushing it back over his shoulders to trace the lines of muscle with quivering fingertips, pressing her lips into the wiry curl of body hair in feverish little kisses. He was so strong, so taut, so totally and completely male. There could never be any other man to match him. Not for her.

When he sat back at last to unfasten his belt, she was past all reckoning. She cried out when he came into her, then everything dissolved into one great spinning vortex and rockets went off in her head.

The storm centre had moved off when she finally began to be aware of discomfort. Brad was lying with one leg thrown across her, a hand heavy on her breast. She could feel his breath on her cheek.

'Cold?' he asked softly as she stirred.

'A bit,' she acknowledged, equally softly.

'You'd better get dressed,' he said, and lifted himself away from her to edge between the front seats and provide her with room to move. 'A chill's the last thing you need.'

What she did need was a few words of reassurance that what had just happened between them had meant as much to him as it had to her, but she obviously wasn't about to get them. She struggled into her clothing again with heavy heart. Nothing had changed. Brad had simply taken advantage of a weakness she hadn't been able to hide from him. Just how long was she going to go on hoping and dreaming?

'I suppose,' she said bitterly to his unresponsive back, 'I asked for that.'

He turned his head to look at her, his expression impossible to read in the renewed darkness. 'I suppose you did.'

'At least any debt I owed you should be paid in full!' she shot back at him, galvanised by his apparent lack of emotion. 'Account closed.'

His sigh was heavy. 'You just don't know when to keep your mouth shut, do you, Kerry? What happened just now happened because we *both* wanted it.'

'A straightforward lust, no other feeling involved—is that what you're trying to say?'

'Where you're concerned, there's nothing straightforward!' he came back on a suddenly savage note. 'You've been giving me hell since the minute I saw you on that plane. Why do you think I was so all-fired eager to keep you off the site?'

Kerry was silent for a moment, not at all certain of her ground. 'I thought it was on account of the men.'

'That was part of the objection. It still is. Introducing a woman into that sort of set-up is like putting a detonator in a powder keg. You spelled trouble all the way down the line.'

She said huskily, 'It was never my intention to get involved with you again, Brad. It cost me too much the last time.'

'You were just a kid,' he said. 'You didn't even know what it was about.'

'I'm not a kid now.'

'Not physically, perhaps.'

It took her a moment or two to absorb that particular hurt. 'I suppose Rina satisfies the complete man,' she said unsteadily, at length.

He shrugged. 'Maybe she does.'

'But you've still no intention of marrying her?'

'No.' His tone was flat. 'I've no intention of marrying anybody.'

'Just take your pleasures where you find them, and to hell with everything else!'

'If you like.' He looked at the luminous dial of his watch. 'We've about two hours till first light. We should try and sleep again.'

'Just stay away from me this time,' she jerked out. 'I don't want you touching me again!'

'Unfortunately, there isn't room to avoid it,' he came back hardily, 'I'm not sitting up here for the next two hours, and that's for sure!'

Kerry lay down without another word. She didn't stir a muscle when he eased in behind her, but there was no shutting out the anguish that was in her heart. If they ever did reach the site again she would have to leave. Right now, the job took second place to the need for escape.

Dawn found her still awake. She rose stiffly as soon as Brad himself began to stir, opening the rear door to a world wreathed in mist. While this lasted there was no chance of setting off anywhere, she thought hollowly, trying to ignore the hunger pangs. Mid-morning yesterday was the last time she had eaten, with at least another fifteen or sixteen hours to go before she could be sure of another meal. It was said that the first twenty-four hours were the worst. After that the stomach stopped craving. She could only hope it was true.

'It will lift as soon as the sun gets high enough,' said Brad, emerging from the car in her wake. 'Shouldn't be long.' He ran a hand over his jaw, grimacing at the rasp of beard. 'At least we can get cleaned up while we wait. There's a spring over there somewhere.'

Kerry glanced at him. 'You've been up here before this, then?'

'Once,' he said. 'Some time ago. The track was dodgy even in the dry season. Anyway, it's sealed off for all time now.' He was already moving in the direction of the spring. 'Coming?'

To refuse would be a futile gesture, she acknowledged. Washing without soap would be difficult, but better than nothing. And a drink might help take the edge off her hunger.

The limestone had absorbed all sign of the rain, but the tiny yellow flowers clothing the rocky outcrop above the spring looked flattened and dashed. Oblivious of the chill still in the air, Brad stripped off his shirt and knelt at the poolside to wash.

A long graze ran across one tanned shoulder, Kerry saw. Odd she hadn't felt it last night. But then her mind had been on other things, she thought cynically. So had his, if it came to that.

'That looks painful,' she said.

He turned, water dripping from him, to reach for his shirt and use it as a towel. 'I'll live. Stay around here while I take a look back at the Land Rover. There may be something we can make use of.'

Rising from her own primitive ablutions, Kerry felt the first touch of warmth like a caress on her bare shoulders as the sun came breaking through. The mist lifted, revealing a sky of pale, luminous blue. Mountains circled the horizon.

From here, the little stream dropped away down a series of rough, boulder-strewn steps towards the next ridge. It didn't look too difficult a route. In sunlight, the village itself was simply a jumble of old stone, devoid of all spookiness. It was doubtful if human foot would ever tread this ground again after they left.

She was ready and waiting when Brad came back up from the car. He had found a box of matches. All they needed now, he said, was something to cook!

'We might find some prickly pear or even plaintains lower down,' he added. 'There's nothing edible round here for sure—unless you fancy snake?'

Kerry shuddered. 'I'd have to be desperate for that!'

'A few more hours and you may be.' His eyes were assessing the route they had to take. 'Let's get started.'

He went first, sure-footed as he negotiated the tumbled boulders. Kerry followed more slowly. He had brought the wheelbrace along with him, too, she noted. Some kind of defence against animal attack, perhaps. Viewed from the rear, he looked powerful enough to tackle anything. She ached with the longing to be safe and secure in his arms again. Not that it would mean anything to him beyond the immediate satisfaction. Not even Rina could lay claim to his inner emotions, it seemed.

That first couple of hours were the best of the day. By nine o'clock the sun's heat was already becoming a burden. The ridge revealed a steep slope covered in rocky piles of limestone heaped like more ruins. The going was rough, the footing treacherous. Brad had to hand her down the worst bits. Things should be better once they reached the tree line, he said. If only, Kerry thought, she didn't feel so utterly bone-weary.

The gorge into which the stream eventually disappeared was too steep to descend, forcing them to detour along the rim to find a less risky path, then work their way back to pick up the stream again lower down. It was there they came across the first clump of fruiting prickly pear.

Getting to the fruit was no simple task. Brad knocked the globes off the ears of the cactus with a twig, then rolled them around in the dirt to break off the spines before peeling them with a pocket-knife he carried. They tasted delicious: a cross in both texture and flavour between a peach and a grape. Hardly satisfying, though, even after a dozen or more. Kerry found herself craving for one of Joe's doorstep sandwiches.

Noon had come and gone before they finally reached the tree line. Heedless of any reptile life which might be in the area, Kerry sank gratefully to a seat in the shade when Brad indicated they should rest.

'We're not going to make it before dark, are we?' she said on a note of resignation.

He gave her a shrewd glance. 'Don't go soft on me now. If we don't make it today, we'll do it tomorrow.'

'By which time they'll probably have search parties out for us!'

'Ten to one it's going to be thought that we took off together for the weekend and got held up,' he said dispassionately. 'There won't be any search parties.'

It could have been worse, she thought. She might have been out here alone. The very notion sent a tremor through her.

'It isn't going to be easy to live this down,' she murmured ruefully.

'You'll survive.' Brad had his head back against a tree trunk, and his eyes were closed. 'You might even benefit from the experience.'

She said it with purpose. 'Which experience?'

His eyes came open again, but revealed no expression as he studied her. 'It would have taken a saint to turn down what you were offering last night, and I was never that.'

'And one woman is as good as another!' she flashed. 'After all, if you hadn't been with me you'd have been with Rina.'

'Let's leave Rina out of it,' he returned shortly. 'In fact, let's just forget the whole subject. Ten minutes and we go, so make the most of it.'

Kerry choked back the words which rose to her lips. He was so detached, so untouchable, but it didn't stop her wanting him. She only wished it could.

CHAPTER NINE

BY MID-AFTERNOON, Kerry was sure she could go no further. Every muscle in her body ached with equal intensity. Brad allowed no more than a five-minute rest every hour, forcing her back on her feet again.

Keeping close to the stream bed was becoming more and more difficult. There were ravines to negotiate along the way, some of them impossible to detour around. For every kilometre gained in distance, Kerry reckoned they were expending effort enough for three or even four. Not that Brad seemed to feel the strain.

Her jeans were standing up to the rigours of the journey better than his thin cotton trousers though. Torn in many places, the original pale fawn colour just about obliterated, they provided little protection. There was blood on one leg from a gash sustained during a hazardous semi-slide down a scree slope. He had torn a strip from the bottom of his shirt to bind it, and since then ignored it, although it must be giving him pain. Jaw dark and rough with a day's growth of beard, hair combed only by his fingers, he looked almost piratical. What she must look like herself, Kerry tried not to imagine. Her hair felt like a bird's nest.

Bird life abounded. She had long ago given up counting the different varieties. A small herd of black, pig-like creatures Brad called *javelinas* were the only animals they saw. The latter gave off a strong, musky scent which lingered in the air even after they were out of sight.

'Most animals will get out of the way if they hear you coming,' he said during one of their stops. 'And we're making enough noise to rouse an army. There's more risk from bears than cats, although they'll usually only attack if they're provoked.'

'You seem to know a lot about it,' Kerry observed.

He shook his head. 'I'm no woodsman. My life revolves around contracting programmes.'

'The job before everything.' There was just the slightest edge to her voice. 'An outlook I aim to adopt for myself.'

'Including marriage?'

She said slowly, 'There's no wedding arranged yet.'

'Meaning you're still not sure you found the right man.' The shrug was brief. 'Plenty of other fish in the sea.'

'So typical of your way of thinking!' she retorted with bitterness. 'Who's going to be *your* next catch?'

Grey eyes registered a sudden spark. 'Cut out the bleeding heart. Anything you've got you've asked for!'

'I suppose that goes for Rina, too?'

'I said to leave her out of it.' He had come away from the rock where he had been leaning his back, and his whole demeanour had hardened. 'About time we were moving, anyway. Another couple of hours and it's going to be dark.'

There was no give in him at all. Kerry wondered bleakly if any woman would ever reach him down deep where it hurt.

The sun was close to setting when they reached the head of the gorge for which they were aiming. Tinged with gold, the dam wall was a thing of beauty and grace, so near and yet so far. Brad found a small cave cut into the rockface, making sure it was empty before allowing her to crawl inside. The dried grass on the floor seemed to indicate that it might have been used by some animal in the past, but there was no scent left now. Tired as she was, it felt almost cosy.

'Your bra straps are elastic, aren't they?' he asked as she lowered herself thankfully to a seat. His lips widened briefly at the look she shot him. 'I used to be a dab hand with a catapult. If I can rig one, I might be able to get us a rabbit. Worth a try, wouldn't you say?'

'I suppose so.' She gave him a steady stare. 'I'll hand it out to you.'

Whatever his thoughts, he kept them to himself. 'I'll go and light a fire,' he said.

The first flames were already licking up through the dried grass and twigs when she put her head outside again. Brad fed in larger pieces of wood, waiting until they had well and truly caught alight before easing himself to his feet to take the proffered garment from her.

'A regular Boy Scout, aren't you?' she jeered when he took the penknife from his jacket pocket to cut the straps away from their anchoring points. 'Always prepared!'

'Stow it,' he advised without looking her way. 'I'm not in the mood.'

Biting her lip, she watched him knot the free ends about the points of a suitably forked stick, then test the makeshift weapon with a small piece of rock aimed at a spiky yucca on the canyon rim.

'Good enough,' he judged. He picked up several more pieces of rock and slid them into a pocket. 'You might gather some more wood while you're waiting. There's plenty lying around.'

Kerry refrained with an effort from begging him not to leave her alone. The fire was some safeguard against the fast-approaching night. By this time tomorrow they would be safely back on site. If that thought no longer stirred her, it was only because she was so utterly weary and depressed.

Darkness had fallen before he returned. She heard him before she saw him, her heart in her throat until the familiar figure emerged into the firelight. He was carrying a fair-sized rabbit by its hindlegs.

'Lucky shot,' he said dismissively when she congratulated him. 'It's been a long time.'

Skinning and paunching the animal with a penknife took time. Only when the carcass was spitted above the flames and beginning to send out a mouth-watering aroma could Kerry bring herself to view it with anything approaching objectivity.

The hunger came back with full force. She could hardly wait to sink her teeth into the roasted flesh when Brad finally pronounced the meal ready. Nothing, she thought, had ever tasted so good!

'How long do you think it will take us to reach the dam?' she asked, when the last bones had been picked clean and her stomach no longer had that terrible hollowness.

'Depends how direct a route we can find round the rim,' he said. 'Two or three hours, maybe.'

'No chance of our sneaking in without anyone noticing, I suppose?'

'Hardly. They'll see us from the dam head.' He waited a moment before tagging on, 'Making it at all is the main thing.'

'I know.' She made a small wry gesture. 'I'd still be up there if you hadn't followed me.'

'I don't want your gratitude.' His tone had hardened again.

'Well, you're getting it regardless!' There was a brief, electric pause. When she broke it there was an ineradicable tremor in her voice. 'Why does it always have to finish up like this between us?'

A breath of wind stirred the glowing embers, the sudden leap of flame highlighting taut features. 'Because you're driving me crazy,' he said. 'Because you're who you are, and I'm who I am.'

She said huskily, 'I'm not sure what that's supposed to mean.'

He turned his head to look at her then, the firelight flickering in his eyes. 'It means we're as incompatible as they come!'

Her pulses quickened, sending waves through her body. 'We needn't be. Not if you stopped resenting me quite so much.'

'Resenting you?' His laugh was short. 'I suppose that's one way of putting it. I had my life all mapped out before you came back on the scene.'

There was a hard obstruction in her throat. 'You're saying I'm different from Rina?'

'Rina and I don't have anything going for us. Not that way. She isn't over her marriage break-up yet.'

It took her a moment to assimilate that. 'I didn't realise she was married,' was all she could find to say.

'She won't be for much longer. Not unless he has a change of heart and comes to get her. She makes more money from her artwork than he does at his job. Apparently he couldn't take it. She even contemplated giving up painting until I talked her out of it.'

'Why?'

'Because no relationship based on that kind of sacrifice is going to work out. If they do get back together at all, it has to be because he's got wise to the kind of fool he's being.'

Kerry said softly, 'You mean you wouldn't feel the same way in the same position?'

'Not over money.'

She wanted badly to know if he had slept with Rina, but the words wouldn't come. Perhaps better to leave it alone. The main thing was his lack of emotional involvement with the American woman—if it were really true.

'Did you ever contemplate marriage at all?' she asked with a certain diffidence, and saw his lips twist.

'Once.'

'What happened?'

'She was too young for me.'

Her heart was beating right up into her throat, the sound of it filling her ears. 'She's older now.'

'Older, maybe, but still not right.'

'Why?' It was all she could do to get the word out.

'Because we both have our own lives to lead.'

'But along similar paths. Surely that makes a difference?'

'It makes it impossible.' His jaw was set. 'What kind of marriage would it be where both partners were in opposite camps?'

'It could be worked out.' Kerry could hardly believe this conversation was actually taking place. 'Providing the incentive was there. If we both felt enough to make the effort...'

'It would take more than effort.'

'Organisation, then. It's up to Dad, remember, as to which construction tender is accepted. Where this kind of job is concerned, he'd always go for KDC. That means I could be part of the consulting team.'

'With the ability to stay objective about the job?' he shook his head. 'It wouldn't work.'

She gazed into the fire, her heart heavy again. He hadn't used the word love, but there had to be some deeper feeling involved for him to talk this way at all. 'Supposing I gave it up?' she said on a low note. 'The job, I mean.'

'That's the last thing I'd want.'

'Then what *do* we do?' It was a cry of sheer frustration.

'I'm going to put the fire out,' he said. 'There's no knowing where the sparks might fly.'

He fetched water from the stream to do it, using a hollowed-out rock as a carrier. The darkness that descended after the last red glow was extinguished seemed more intense. Kerry waited for her eyes to adjust, with her gaze riveted on the tall, dark shape. What she'd felt for him when she was eighteen hadn't been love. Not as she knew it now. She wasn't about to let it go because of some possible future problems that could surely be resolved.

'Make love to me,' she said softly, and saw his teeth gleam white for an instant.

'I intend to. A final indulgence while the opportunity's still there.'

'It doesn't have to be final,' she insisted as he drew her to her feet. 'I love you, Brad!'

He was silent for a moment, his expression impossible to read. When he spoke his voice had a cynical note. 'When exactly did you decide that?'

'I didn't have to decide it. I've been fighting it ever since we met up again.' Heedless of the roughness, she put both hands along his jawline to draw down his face to within reach of her lips, kissing him with a kind of desperation. 'I'm not engaged to Tim. I only said it to stop Glenn from getting any ideas. I never felt anything much for anyone after you. You have to believe that!'

He made no answer. Hands buried in her hair, he held her to a kiss that stirred her every sense. She could feel the iron in him still, but there was a softer core in there somewhere, and she was going to find it.

Small as it was, the cave held the two of them comfortably. Brad spread both jackets on the floor before laying her down, resting on his side to run a slow, exploratory hand down the length of her body, leaving no part of her untouched.

'Now I know how a blind man must feel,' he murmured. 'I've never seen you in daylight.'

'Nor I you, if it comes to that,' she said. She rolled towards him as emotion swept her, wanting his heat, his hardness, his assurance. His skin tasted faintly salty, the hair tickling her lips. She pressed herself feverishly against him, hardly able to contain the sheer, heady desire as she felt his instant response.

'Not yet,' he said softly. 'This has to last.'

Cupping each breast from beneath, he bent his head to run his tongue over the tender, peaking flesh, rousing her to a pitch where nothing else existed but that flickering, tormenting source of pleasure. His hands were experienced, knowing just where to touch, where to linger...how to stay her on the very brink.

Taking wasn't enough. She had to know him the same way. There was no surplus flesh on him, each and every muscle clearly defined. His thighs were as firm and hard as young tree-trunks, the hair on them softer than that on his chest. His breathing roughened and his stomach muscles tensed, the fingers threaded through her hair tightening in involuntary spasm. Steel wrapped in velvet, she thought mistily, and all hers!

She was mindless with wanting when he finally came to her. She spread supple limbs to receive him, blood racing like liquid fire through her veins as he drove to the very centre of her being, back arching in ecstasy to the feel of him, the power of him, the sheer, head-spinning, mind-melting rapture of possessing and being possessed. Nothing could be allowed to come between them, came the last fading thought. Not after this!

She must have fallen asleep immediately afterwards. When she opened her eyes again there was light filtering into the cave. Brad's jacket and her own shirt were draped across her, but he was gone. Perhaps to try and find food, she told herself, luxuriating for a moment in the memory of last night's lovemaking. Right now she could have eaten a horse!

Warm water and soap were another priority, she acknowledged, struggling with distaste into her soiled clothing. Her hair had knots in it that her fingers couldn't get through. It was only to be hoped they would come out when it was wet. Short hair didn't suit her face.

Brad had a fire going, and a bird about the size of a bantam hen already roasting on it when she got outside. The grey eyes were enigmatic.

'I went looking for prickly pear and got lucky again,' he said. 'Knocked it right off its roost.'

Silly to allow sentiment to creep in, Kerry conceded. They were still several hours' trek from journey's end. An empty stomach was no good start.

On impulse, she went to him, sliding her arms about his waist from the back to press her cheek against his shirt. 'I love you,' she whispered. 'How do you feel about me?'

There was no response in him—or none that she could feel, at any rate. 'It's pretty immaterial,' he said.

'No, it isn't!' She refused to be put off her stride. 'You couldn't have made love to me the way you did last night if you didn't feel *something*!'

He freed her arms from about his waist to bring her round in front of him, his grasp far from gentle. 'We already went through all that.'

'Not with any far-reaching conclusions.' Kerry searched the firm features, but her heart plummeted sickeningly at the cool, clear purpose in his eyes. 'Brad, we can't just leave it like this!'

'We not only can, but we're going to,' he said. 'We both have other interests.'

'Not as important as this.'

There was no softening of expression. 'That's where we differ. My job is my life.'

'It could be *our* life—together.' She was trying hard not to plead. 'You love me, Brad. I *know* you do!'

His lips twisted. 'Depends what you mean by love. I've managed without you so far, I guess I can go on doing it. I'd better rescue that bird before it cremates.'

She watched him helplessly as he went back to the fire. He meant what he said, that was obvious. So far as he was concerned, there was no future for them. There would be no changing his mind; she knew him well enough for that. Whatever dreams she had entertained, she could forget them.

The anger seizing her was a defence against the pain. She wanted to lash out at him—to penetrate that hardened shell and hurt him the way he was hurting her. 'You really are a prize louse!' she said with icy control. 'And I'm a fool for ever doubting it!'

He didn't even turn his head. 'So having got that sorted out, let's eat,' he said. 'I'd like to be back on site before lunch.'

Delicious as the roast fowl both smelled and tasted, Kerry had to force herself to swallow it. By the time they were ready to set off on what was hopefully the last lap of the journey, she had her emotions in hand, although the dull heaviness in her chest showed no sign of dispersing.

Cleared from the bottom half of the gorge, the trees clustered thickly about the upper slopes. Picking her way in Brad's wake along narrow animal trails as likely to peter out as lead anywhere, Kerry wondered why they hadn't simply climbed down into the gorge and followed the river through to the dam wall.

'Because the rockface is sheer to either side of it,' he said when she finally put the question to him. 'And we're not equipped for climbing. We'll get there eventually.'

To face what? she thought. The way she had felt on waking, she could have walked on site without a care in the world, but not any more. Nobody was going to believe the truth of the story for a moment. It would probably be assumed that she and Brad had arranged to meet up there in the mountains, and had been caught by the landslide. She wasn't sure she was going to be able to take it. Not with people like Pete Lomas around to throw in his contribution. Yet to leave now would only lend weight to speculation.

Except that if she were gone it wouldn't matter to her, would it? Brad wouldn't give a damn what was being said. Several more weeks of seeing him every day was beyond her to contemplate, anyway. Back home she could reorganise her life—restore incentive. Tim would have to be told, of course. Marriage with him was out of the question. She would take a leaf out of Brad's book and make her job the be-all-and-end-all of existence.

Oh, God, she thought miserably, if only it were that simple!

It was near ten o'clock when they finally made the dam. Emerging from the trees at last to see the men at work on the top was almost an anticlimax. Someone spotted them descending the slight slope towards the road, and drew the attention of those in the immediate vicinity. Brad paid little heed to the watchers, heading for one of the vehicles parked at the dam head.

'We may as well ride the rest of the way,' he said. 'We'll let Alan Pope know you're OK, then go and get cleaned up.'

They found the resident engineer and Glenn together. The former was the first to give voice to the feelings they both displayed facially.

'Thank God you're safe! What on earth happened?'

Kerry left it to Brad to do the talking. She felt oddly detached, as if she were watching a scene in a play. What he actually said she had no clear idea. A great weariness had settled over her. All she wanted was to be alone.

Glenn was looking at her oddly. The same way, she didn't doubt, that everyone else would be looking. She felt detached from that prospect, too. Only when Brad indicated they should leave did she gather her wits enough to give the man at the desk a rueful glance.

'Sorry about this, Alan. I should have had more sense.'

'We'll talk about it later,' he said. 'Right now you need to rest.'

They were at the camp before Brad spoke again. 'I'll get Joe to send you some food over as soon as you're through.'

'I'm not hungry,' she replied truthfully. 'I'd rather just get some sleep.'

'Fair enough.' He obviously wasn't prepared to argue about it. 'Just give me a knock when you get back from the shower-house.'

It took her bare moments to gather soap and towel and the white overalls. Brad's door was firmly closed when she passed. The row of basins in the shower-house had damp-spotted mirrors above them. She viewed her reflection without emotion.

Difficult to believe any man could find her attractive at present. Her face looked pinched, her eyes lacklustre, her skin sallow. Her hair was a wild tangle, with bits of last night's dried grass still caught up in it. Taking up her brush, she attacked it with force, only desisting when the last knot was gone. Washed, it should be as good as new. A pity she couldn't wash out the last fortnight as easily.

There were several open shower stalls, each with its own control. Standing under the jet of warm water, she soaped herself all over twice before feeling really clean again. She was rinsing her hair when the sound of the outer door opening and closing impinged on her consciousness. Footsteps came across the wooden floor. Her towel out of reach, she shrank to the back of the stall, her breath coming out on a gasp that was part relief, part anger when Brad came into view.

'You were gone so long I thought something had happened to you,' he said.

She straightened jerkily to squeeze out the wet strands, refusing to show what she was feeling. 'I'm through now.'

Her towel was hung on a hook outside the stall. He moved to get it, wrapping it about her like a cocoon. It took everything she had to stop herself from twisting into his arms. Whatever he felt for her, it wasn't love. Not as she understood the word.

'Just leave me alone,' she gritted. 'You've had everything you're going to get from me!'

For a moment his hands tightened on her shoulders, then he released her abruptly. 'You're right,' he said. 'There's no point in prolonging things.'

She felt him move away, heard the rasp of a zip as he began to shed his soiled clothing. Unable to contemplate crossing the compound dressed only in a towel, she kept her back turned while she finished drying herself, and got into the white overalls.

To reach the door, she had to pass by the shower stall Brad was using. Despite keeping her gaze rigidly to the front, she could still see the tall, muscular body on the periphery of her vision—still feel the same aching need to be close to him again. She would get over him. The same way she had got over him four years ago.

Only she hadn't, had she? Right through university he'd been there at the back of her mind, making her fellow students seem so immature by comparison. Well, to hell with him! she told herself fiercely. She'd be damned if she'd spend the rest of her life hankering after any man!

Safe in her room again, she finished rubbing her hair dry, then lay down on the bed to rest and contemplate the immediate future. Brad would no doubt be back on the job after the lunch-break. Perhaps she should do the same. Whatever she had to face, it was surely better than skulking in here for the rest of the day.

When she opened her eyes the light had changed from the full white glare of midday to a softer glow. The knock that had aroused her came again on the door. Still not fully awake, she staggered to her feet and went to answer it, looking with blank expression at the man standing outside.

'Alan suggested I come over and make sure you were all right,' said Glenn. 'Sorry if I woke you.'

Kerry forced the fog from her mind with an effort. 'What time is it?' she asked.

'Just before three.' He was obviously at something of a loss over what to say next. 'Have you eaten at all?'

She shook her head, half expecting him to produce a plate from behind his back.

'Would you like me to fetch you something?'

About to refuse, she hesitated. Food was necessary to physical if not mental well-being, and her stomach certainly felt empty. 'I wouldn't mind some coffee and a sandwich,' she acknowledged. 'If you're sure you don't mind?'

'Of course not.' He was already moving. 'Ten minutes.'

She made haste to get into some clothes while he was gone. Slept on while still damp, her hair felt rough. She drew it back into the nape of her neck with a tortoiseshell slide and left it at that. Glenn was the last person she needed to impress.

The sandwiches he returned with were of Joe's special variety, but she was too hungry by then to care how thick and ungainly they were.

'Thanks,' she said gratefully, taking the tray from him. 'Will you tell Alan I'll be there in a little while?'

Glenn looked surprised. 'I think he took it for granted you'd be taking the rest of the day to recover. I only came to check on you.'

'If I sleep any more,' she said, 'I'm not going to do it tonight. Anyway, I'd as soon get it over with.' She added on wryly, 'I imagine he had some pretty choice comments to make.'

The smile was a little uncomfortable. 'It was a shock for him to realise how close you'd come to not being here at all. For both of us, if it comes to that. Until I saw Rina in town yesterday, I'd taken it for granted you were at her place.' He paused briefly, his expression revealing. 'You *and* Brad. Lucky he saw you go.'

'I was a fool,' Kerry admitted. 'I should have known better. Brad thinks the insurance will cover the cost of replacements for both Land Rovers. Does it sound likely under the circumstances?'

'If he says it is then I imagine it is.' Glenn sounded just faintly ironic. 'Would you like me to wait and run you back to the office?'

'Would you?' she asked. 'My calf muscles feel as if they've been kicked!'

'Hardly surprising, considering the kind of country you had to come through. It must have been tough going.'

Not all of it, she thought bleakly, making the appropriate noises. The toughest part of all was going to be forgetting.

CHAPTER TEN

ALAN greeted her with reticence. 'You certainly don't do things by halves,' he said. 'Just try to stay out of trouble from now on, will you?'

Either that, Kerry gathered, reading between the lines, or just go on home. She had been ready to do just that a few hours ago. Now that she had slept on it, the feeling had passed. Brad or no Brad, she had to prove herself. This was the only life she wanted, the life she was determined to have. Nothing else was going to matter.

The rain came in a solid deluge around five, although minus the theatrical effects of Saturday night. With the whole site turned to a sea of mud, and finishing-time so close, work was abandoned for the day.

'I think we can say the season finally got under way,' Glenn observed, peering through the streaming windscreen as they drove back to base. 'Pity it couldn't have held off for another couple of weeks, but that's how it goes. At least it doesn't normally last all that long.' He cast Kerry a glance. 'Coming over to the rec. after supper?'

She shook her head. 'I think I'll settle for an early night.'

'Understandable.' His pleasant features had clouded a little. 'You've had a pretty rough weekend.'

'It could have been worse.' She added lightly, 'Any idea yet where your next job will be, Glenn?'

'Depends on what your father has lined up,' he said.

'Something closer to home, perhaps?'

He shrugged. 'I'd only make that a priority if I had good reason.'

'What would you call good reason?'

'A wife, for one. Not many marriages survive long separation. Anyway, the problem hasn't arisen yet. Perhaps it never will. Some men are destined for bachelordom.'

'Not you.' She said it with conviction. 'You've a whole lot to offer the right girl.'

A faint smile touched his lips. 'Not enough.'

The implication was too obvious for comment. A simple matter of propinquity, Kerry assured herself. Once out of sight, she would soon be out of mind.

There was no sign of Brad in the canteen later. It was possible, she reflected, that he'd gone to make his explanations to Rina. Whatever story he told the American woman, it almost certainly wouldn't include the more intimate details. Whether she would suspect the truth or not was something else.

Kerry was glad to escape the knowing glances directed her way. Her room was the only haven she had left. She read magazines for a while, though with little real interest. By nine o'clock she was ready to scream from sheer boredom and frustration.

With everyone else across at the recreation room, she could at least get some air in peace. She went to get her jacket from the wardrobe, pushing aside the poncho still hanging there. It would have to be returned, of course, but not by her. Let Brad take it back.

She could see his door was open before she reached it. What she hadn't expected was to see him lounging on his bed, with his hands clasped comfortably behind his head.

'Going across to the rec.?' he asked as their eyes met.

'Hardly,' she returned. 'I had enough of the speculation at dinner.'

'Just talk.' He sounded unmoved. 'If it bothers you all that much the solution is obvious.'

'I'm not leaving,' she stated flatly. 'I take it you've been down to see Rina?'

'That's right.'

'What did you tell her?'

'The truth,' he said. 'Minus the personal detail, of course.'

'Oh, of course. After all, you wouldn't want to risk your home comforts for the next few weekends!'

'I've told you before,' he came back expressionlessly, 'it isn't that kind of relationship.'

'Where you're concerned, there *is* only one kind.' It was becoming increasingly difficult to keep her emotions at bay. 'You were right about one thing. We don't have any future together. I must have been crazy even to consider it!'

Something flickered in the grey eyes, but he still made no move. 'Glad we're agreed on that score, at least.'

It was time to go, Kerry thought numbly, yet to continue with her original aim meant passing this way again on return. The sudden hammering of rain on the tin roof was a godsend.

'Looks like I'll have to forgo the constitutional,' she said. 'Goodnight, Brad.'

She was moving before he answered, too close to giving herself away to linger any longer. Reaching her room again, she closed the door and stood there for a moment with eyes closed and chest tight. She could still see his image behind her lids, lounging there untouched by even the merest hint of regret. He wasn't worth what she was going through, she tried to tell herself, but it didn't help.

The season settled down to a fairly predictable pattern over the following few days. With the rain mostly confined to the late afternoon and early evening, work went on apace. There was talk of closing the sluice gates by the end of the next week. After that it would just be a case of finishing off.

For Kerry the evenings were the worst time. She could keep both mind and body busy during the day, but once dinner was over the hours dragged. Even Glenn seemed to have distanced himself a little. Although still convinced of the temporary nature of his attachment, she felt a certain responsibility for it. Deprived of any emotional outlet for so many months, and too decent to seek the kind of relief some of the other men sought, he had been ready to fall for the first girl he laid eyes on. She should have realised that from the start.

Where Brad was concerned, there was no contact at all. The men themselves appeared to have lost interest in the subject of their supposed association, although certainly not in her. She was never going to be accepted as one of the boys, even metaphorically speaking, she conceded, but refused to allow that knowledge to undermine her determination. She was as capable of doing this job as any man, and therefore entitled to be granted an equal opportunity. Let anyone try to take that away from her!

Saturday found her at something of a loss. Neither Alan nor anyone else had said anything about going down to town, although she could hardly imagine they were all planning to spend the whole weekend on the site. Asking for the loan of another Land Rover was obviously out of the question. With two still missing, transport must be in short supply as it was. Joining the men on the trucks was one solution, but it would be asking for trouble to think of returning that way. Pete Lomas was drawback enough.

As was usual, she left the office ahead of everyone else in order to use the facilities before the main force arrived. Someone would be going down to Las Meridas this afternoon, there was no doubt. If getting back proved to be a problem, she could always book in to one of the two hotels. Despite what Brad had said about them, they looked clean enough from outside.

Showered, and wearing the khaki trouser suit, she was stringing up the items of underwear she had washed through when the knock came on the door. Half expecting to find Glenn standing there, she was nonplussed to meet grey eyes instead of hazel.

'I'll be ready to leave in fifteen minutes,' he said.

Kerry found her voice again, unsurprised by its tinny sound. 'To go where?'

'The same place we should have gone last week.'

Her head came up, jaw firming. 'I don't think so.'

'I'm not asking you,' Brad came back flatly. 'I'm telling you. I've Alan Pope's backing to pack you out by force if necessary!'

'It isn't his place,' she retorted with a coolness she was far from feeling. 'Any more than it's *your* business. I'd as soon take my chances right here.'

'I just told you,' he said, 'you don't have a choice. Rina's expecting you. This time you don't let her down.'

'How do you think I'm going to feel accepting her hospitality after what happened last week?' she appealed, trying a new tack.

'It won't be the first time.' His mouth slanted briefly at the look in her eyes. 'Providing it doesn't happen under her roof, what's the odds?'

'To you, obviously nothing, but it matters to me!'

'You're still going.' His voice held a growing impatience. 'Unless you'd rather I ran you straight on through to Ciudad and put you on a bus for Monterrey, seeing there isn't another flight out until Monday. One or the other, Kerry. The only choice you don't have is spending the night up here.'

He was moving away before she could say anything else. Not that there was much she could say, she thought painfully. It would relieve the whole situation if she went on to Monterrey, but she couldn't bring herself to accept that way out. Which left her with only one course.

Her things were already packed against the likelihood that she had to spend the night down in the town, anyway. By the time Brad returned, she was ready, if not willing, to accompany him out to the waiting car.

The hooter signalling the end of the week's work was just sounding as he switched on the ignition. At least there was no one around to prejudge the situation, she reflected with cynicism. A further flare-up of speculation was the last thing she needed.

'Any joy on the replacements yet?' she asked stiffly as they headed out.

Brad shook his head. 'It's doubtful if there'll be any this close to completion. We were over actual requirements to start with. We'll just manage now with what we've got.'

'But the insurance will cover?'

'Looks like it.' He gave her a brief glance. 'Scared you might have to face your father with the bill?'

'Concerned,' she corrected. 'I've never had cause to be scared of Dad.'

'You're going to tell him about your little jaunt, then?'

'I'm sure if I don't you'll make sure he hears about it!'

'Not my style,' he denied.

Kerry bit her lip. A waste of time trying to get at him that way. His closeness in the confines of the vehicle was telling on her. She was vividly aware of the lean strength in his hands on the wheel, of the taut muscularity in the thigh almost brushing hers. She wanted him so desperately to stop the car, to pull her forcefully into his arms, to kiss her into that state of oblivion where nothing else counted but the here and now. If she asked him to make love to her again he might even do it, but there would still be no future in it. Once a lone wolf, always a lone wolf.

Another attitude she might cultivate for herself if she wanted to make her career all-important, came the thought. No commitments, no deep involvement. Or better still, train herself to do without men altogether. Other women managed to survive.

'Do you plan on staying with KDC?' she asked, trying to find a level at which they could communicate without stress.

'Depends,' he said. 'I've been offered a move to home office.'

'Choice, or ultimatum?'

'Supposedly the former.'

'But you're not going to take it?'

He shrugged. 'I'd be troubleshooting, mostly. I'm not sure I'm cut out for it.' He swore under his breath as they rounded a bend to see broken rock scattered across the surface of the road. 'Happens every time it rains!'

Stopping the car, he got out to clear a path through. Kerry watched him through the windscreen, feeling the ache in her chest deepen. At this time a week ago he had been chasing her into the mountains. If the chance had been offered, she would willingly have re-lived those two days just to be alone with him again. Love was a mug's game, she had told herself at eighteen. It still was.

There was little conversation between them after that. For Kerry herself, the effort of dissimulation was too much. Brad seemed unconcerned by her silence. Stealing the occasional surreptitious glance at the granite profile, she wondered just what it would take to shake him. The loss of his job, perhaps. Not that that was likely. The best agent in the business, Glenn had said. Without his co-ordination, that dam back there would still be only half built.

Rina's greeting was as friendly as ever it had been. She wasn't waiting for it, she claimed, when Kerry apologised for forgetting to bring the poncho with her.

They ate lunch out on the patio, with a bottle of wine to share. Watching the ruby-red liquid sparkle through the glass, feeling the sun's warmth on her back, Kerry had to admit that civilisation had its advantages. As before, Brad himself seemed a different person down here. Rina had a relaxing effect—like the wine they were drinking. It was impossible to stay aloof from her.

'I need some things from the market,' she announced when the dishes had been cleared away. 'Either of you fancy coming?'

Lying stretched out on one of the somewhat battered loungers, soaking up the sun, Brad said lazily, 'I'll give it a miss. We're eating out tonight, by the way. Gustavo is putting on something special.'

Rina laughed. 'With Gustavo, everything is special! The best restaurant in town,' she added for Kerry's benefit. 'Providing you turn a blind eye to the décor.' She paused enquiringly. 'Do you want to stay or come?'

'I'll come,' Kerry responded, turning her back on the fleeting temptation. She and Brad had nothing left to say to each other.

'What made you choose Las Meridas in the first place?' she asked curiously, as they walked down to the plaza. 'It's so far off the beaten track.'

'One of the attractions,' Rina admitted. 'I needed room to breathe. The scenery was another draw. I've an exhibition coming up in a few weeks. I have to have some new canvases ready to show.'

'Any chance of seeing them?'

'You're more than welcome.' She waited a moment before adding evenly, 'It isn't working out with you and Brad, is it?'

Kerry felt her heart give a painful jerk. 'What isn't?'

The laugh came low. 'I'm not dense, honey. You're in love with the guy. Not that I blame you. I might have fallen myself if things had been different.'

'Different in what way?' The words were dragged from her.

'If I weren't still crazy about my husband. He probably isn't half the man Brad is, but I'd jump through hoops to have him back. We're the biggest fools out when it comes to love.' She paused. Then her tone altered. 'Just for the record, on the few occasions Brad has stayed overnight we've occupied different beds. The times you were here, he used the sofa, the same way he will to-night. If we'd slept together it would have ruined a very good friendship—for both of us.'

There was relief in what she was saying, but little con-solation. Jealousy had been a relatively minor issue, anyway. 'I appreciate your telling me,' Kerry acknowl-edged, 'but it doesn't really change anything. Brad isn't interested in any lasting relationship.'

Rina's glance was shrewd. 'It would be pretty difficult to form one, considering the circumstances, wouldn't it? You might both be on different continents this time next year.'

'I know.' Kerry gave a self-deprecating little laugh. 'I even offered to give up my job for him.'

'Would you really want to?'

'No,' she admitted. 'I want the best of both worlds.'

It was Rina's turn to laugh. 'Don't we all!'

They spent a companionable afternoon. Kerry pur-chased an intricately worked silver necklet and matching bracelet, planning to wear both items along with the skirt and blouse she had bought a couple of weeks before. It would be a nice change to dress like a woman again, if only for the one evening.

Coming face to face with Pete Lomas as she fingered through a rail of the long, loose Indian blouses known as *huipil* was an occasion she could have done without. He was with two of the other men, neither of whom looked any too comfortable when he started taunting her.

'Lover-boy found other interests, then? Real shame! If it's another man you're looking for, I'm right here, babe!'

'If it *were* a man I was looking for,' she said coldly, 'you wouldn't even come close!'

His expression turned ugly. 'You're too damned lippy, that's your trouble. One of these days, somebody's going to show you what for!'

'Not you,' she retorted. 'You don't have what it takes!'

'Let's go, Pete,' said one of the other men on a placatory note as he took a step towards her.

There was a moment when it seemed the plea might be ignored, then he shrugged and fell back again. 'You'll get what's coming to you,' he threatened. 'Just see if I'm right!'

Only just arrived on the scene, Rina looked from the retreating backs to Kerry's face with lifted brows. 'What was all that about?'

'One of Brad's crew with a score to settle,' Kerry returned wryly. 'I'm not too good at handling his type.'

'I guess Brad will sort him out.' It was said with confidence. 'Ready to go?'

The sun was already well down when they left the market to make their way up through the narrow backstreets. Bathed in warm golden light, even the shabbiest of buildings took on new life. In some ways the coming affluence would probably spoil the place, Kerry mused. Right now, the town had character—a sense of history. This time next year the invasion would have altered all that. Perhaps it was as well she would be gone before it really started happening.

There was another car parked outside the house, she saw, as they climbed the final slope. A big American sedan. It took Rina's sudden indrawn breath to signify who the owner might be.

The fair-haired, almost too-handsome man sitting with Brad in the living-room got to his feet as the two of them came into the house, his eyes seeking those of his wife with an expression bordering on sheepishness.

'Hi,' he said softly.

'Hi.' Rina's expression was difficult to read. 'You drove all the way down from LA?'

'Four days,' he acknowledged. 'I left Monterrey early this morning.'

'You must have.' She dropped the packages she was carrying on to the nearest chair. 'Kerry, I'd like you to meet my husband. Kerry's an engineer, Leo.'

'So I've been hearing,' with a glance in Brad's direction. 'Must make things a whole lot easier sharing the same basic interests.'

Grey eyes met green, the warning clear to her if not to anyone else. 'You'd better think about getting prettied up if we're going out to that meal. Gustavo tends to lose his touch after the first hour or so.' Brad's glance switched to Rina. 'Leo thought you'd prefer to eat here.'

'Yes,' she said. 'I think we have to.'

Kerry stirred herself to make for the stairs. 'Give me ten minutes,' she managed with creditable composure.

Brad's reasons for implying they were an accepted partnership were only too obvious, of course. Considering the instability of the marriage, Leo might have found a purely platonic relationship between his wife and the man who had opened her door to him as hard to swallow as she herself first had. What she did wonder about was exactly how close she and Brad were supposed to be.

Acting a part or no, his regard when she went down again was flattering in its open approval. Rina was getting a hasty meal together in the kitchen. She gave Kerry an abstracted glance when the latter went in.

'I just wondered if you'd rather be on your own to-night?' she said.

The blonde head moved in a negative gesture. 'Whatever Leo came to say, it will be over and done with by the time you get back.' Her smile lacked its usual spontaneity. 'See you later.'

Leo was sitting with a glass in his hand and a pensive look on his face when they left him. Kerry waited until Brad had started the car before voicing the question.

'Do you think he's looking for a reconciliation?'

'I'd say there's a strong probability,' he responded. 'Nobody drives for four days to ask for a divorce when a letter would do the same job. If they do get back to-gether again, let's hope it's on the right terms. Rina's a damn good artist. She'd be a fool to give it up.' He glanced her way, voice taking on a different note. 'Nice to see you looking feminine again. Pants only look good on a girl for so long.'

'I could hardly go on site dressed like this,' she said. 'It's one of the sacrifices I have to make.'

'It needn't be if you weren't so set on proving a point. How do you reckon on dealing with someone like Lomas, for instance? Because there's sure to be at least one, whatever the job.'

'I'd already put him out of action before you showed yourself,' she rejoined coolly. 'And there's rather more to it than just proving a point. You're not the only one who'd go mad confined to an office all day and every day.'

'Except that I wouldn't be,' he said. 'Even if I did take the move. Neither need you. There's site work attached to every job, big and small.'

'I'm not interested in kennel building,' she came back. 'There's the Lazlo dam in Nigeria. I may get myself involved with that.'

His jaw had tightened. 'If you won't listen to sense, your father will!'

'It isn't your concern!'

'I'm making it my concern. Somebody has to put a spoke in your wheel.'

He wouldn't stop her, Kerry vowed silently, recognising the futility of further discussion. No one was going to stop her!

Gustavo's was just off the main plaza. Containing no more than half a dozen tables in addition to the long serving bar at the rear of the premises, it was already doing a roaring trade. The short, fat Mexican who greeted Brad with such enthusiasm turned out to be Gustavo's brother. An empty table was procured, and handwritten menus presented.

They had *tostadas*, which were crisply fried *tortillas* heaped with chopped vegetables and meat and covered in melted cheese. Delicious, Kerry had to agree, though her appetite wasn't up to finishing the dish. She refused a dessert and settled for coffee, wondering how Rina and Leo were getting on. Nice if one story could have a happy ending, she reflected.

'Was the decision to stay uninvolved mutual?' she asked, without looking at the man seated opposite. 'You and Rina, I mean.'

'A tacit understanding,' he said.

'Hardly your style.'

'How would you know?' His tone was mild enough but with a sardonic underlay. 'To tell the truth, it was a relief to be with a woman I could relax with. I'm not saying I'd have backed off if the offer had been there, but I can't say I've suffered any for lack of it. She's made the weekends worth living these last few months.'

'A pleasure you stand to lose if Leo stays on.'

'All in a good cause. It's doubtful they'll hang around, anyway, if they do make it up.'

'And you'll be leaving yourself before too long,' she finished for him.

'We all will,' he returned.

'Oh, I might not stay out the full term. After all, I was only here to pick up the basics.'

'And you think you've done that?'

This time she did lift her head, meeting the un-revealing gaze with what control of her own she could muster. 'Enough to give me a start.'

He was silent for a long moment, lowering his eyes to the vulnerable hollow of her throat beneath the silver filigree, and sliding his gaze over her bared shoulders. A muscle tautened in his jaw. 'You just don't know when to give up,' he said. 'If KDC get the Nigerian job, there's every likelihood I'll be fronting the team. In that case, there's no way you'll be going!'

'It hasn't even been put out to tender yet,' Kerry re-joined. 'A bit premature, don't you think, to count on anything? It might even be decided to use local con-tractors.' She didn't bother to wait for any reply. 'Is it too soon to go on back? I'm tired.'

Face set, Brad signalled for the bill. The other diners were still only just warming up to the serious business of eating when they left. It wasn't yet ten o'clock, Kerry realised, glancing at her watch as she got into the Land Rover. It was only to be hoped that the other two would have had time to sort out their affairs.

She felt surprisingly unemotional at the moment. Perhaps her feelings didn't run as deep as she had imagined. Brad was angry—she could sense it in him—but that didn't concern her, either. Let him stew.

As always, the house was unlocked. All the same, Brad knocked, waiting several moments before finally opening the door. Apart from the two glasses side by side on the low table, there was no sign of the occupants. They could only be upstairs, Kerry thought, and felt the ache suddenly renewed.

'Looks as if the reconciliation might be on,' she said, hearing the tremor in her voice and hoping Brad wouldn't. 'I'll say goodnight.'

He caught hold of her before she reached the second tread, his hands none too gentle as they swung her round and pulled her to him. There was more than anger in the ruthless pressure of his mouth; he wanted to hurt. She felt suffocated by it, almost ready to pass out through sheer lack of air when he finally lifted his head again.

'Go to bed,' he said grimly. 'I've had all I'm going to take.'

Her throat raw, she turned and left him standing there. It was getting worse, not better.

They left for the site at three, leaving behind a couple whose chances of finding lasting happiness together appeared to be, at the very least, promising.

They would be going back to LA in a couple of days, Rina had said. This time with a better understanding of each other's needs. She wouldn't be giving up her painting, but she would be paying rather more attention to the man she had married. It wasn't just the money angle, she had admitted to Kerry that morning. Her work had begun to take over her whole life.

Brad was withdrawn. With Leo present, his farewells had been necessarily circumspect, but Kerry couldn't help wondering just how much he was going to miss Rina's companionship. He wouldn't be the first to realise his true feelings when it was too late.

There was lightning flickering around the far ridge of mountain-tops when they breasted the last rise. Judging from the build-up of cloud, they were in for yet another of the seasonal storms. At the very least, the run-off over the coming weeks would ensure a swifter achievement of level once the sluices were closed. Seen from that viewpoint, completion couldn't have been better planned.

Few people appeared to have elected to stay on site. It was to be hoped, Brad remarked, that the majority made it back before the storm broke, or there was every likelihood they'd find themselves cut off until morning.

He made no attempt to get out of the car himself when they reached the block. 'I've some paperwork I want to catch up on before morning,' he said. 'I'll be down at the office if anyone wants me.'

Anyone except for her, Kerry thought wryly, going indoors as he turned the Land Rover around and headed out again. What arrangements he might be planning for her the next weekend, she had no idea, though it was doubtful if he would simply sit back and leave her to it. It would be best all round if she made arrangements to leave on the Thursday morning flight. Where was the point in hanging on to the bitter end?

One of the trucks returned about five-thirty. No more than five minutes later, the heavens erupted in a display of such ferocity that Kerry was sure the roof itself was going to cave in. Lightning flashes outlined the landscape in electric blue, while the thunder made the ground itself quiver in sympathy.

It was over in half an hour or so, the rain ceasing as suddenly as it had begun. The familiar smell of wet earth and sodden vegetation permeated the air. Hopefully, Kerry thought, the second truck hadn't been caught on the way up. A storm like that would almost certainly have brought down more rock.

The Sunday evening meal was a casual affair. Those who were back and wanted food could have a cold collation, but relatively few bothered after spending most of the weekend over-indulging in liquid refreshment. Kerry went over with Glenn and a couple of the other consultant staff because, hungry or not, it was better than loafing around in her room, trying to pass the time.

Brad was not in evidence. Whether he was still out at the site or had eaten before they arrived, she had no way of knowing, and no intention of asking. He wasn't in the recreation room, either, when they adjourned there. She played a couple of games of draughts with Glenn, sat through a technical discussion between all three men for what she could learn, and excused herself on the grounds of tiredness around ten o'clock when it became obvious that Brad was not going to put in an appearance.

The second truck was just drawing in as she emerged into the open air. Laughing and shouting, and not a little drunk, the men piled off. There would be some thick heads in the morning, Kerry thought, seeing two of them flounder in the mud left by the storm as they stumbled off the duckboards. Curses rent the air.

'If it isn't the Duchess herself!' intoned an all-too-familiar voice on a slurred note. 'Thinks she's a cut above the likes of us poor slobs!'

Kerry steeled herself to carry on walking as if she hadn't heard the comment. Pete Lomas was bad enough sober. Drunk, he didn't bear thinking about. At least there were others with him. Even he would draw the line at any physical attack under observation.

Except that the chortles coming from those accompanying him sounded more in the nature of encouragement than disapprobation. Unsteady footsteps rattled the boards in her wake; then a hand seized her shoulder, yanking her round to face leering eyes.

'Bad manners to walk away when somebody's talkin' to you,' he admonished. 'Too big for your britches, that's your failin'!'

'Particular about whom I talk to,' she corrected icily, knowing she was adding fuel to the fire yet unable to bring herself to try humouring him, either. 'Take your hands off me!'

The laugh had a nasty edge. 'Not what you said last time, babe. You were really somethin' that night! How about a repeat?'

She tried to twist away, felt her foot slip on the wooden decking and next moment was lying in the mud herself with Pete Lomas on top of her, his beery breath full in her face.

'Just can't wait, can you, babe?' he mocked. 'Just achin' for it!'

Even as she struggled with him, a part of Kerry's mind registered the sudden silence on the part of those

watching the scene. A shadow loomed over the two of
them, and her assailant was plucked from her as one
might have removed a leech. She caught a glimpse of
Brad's face as he held the other man in front of him
with one hand and drew back a clenched fist, his jaw
rigid and his eyes glittering with a savage, unholy light.
Then the bulldozer driver was down on his back and out
for the count.

'See to him,' Brad curtly instructed the by now
thoroughly sobered bystanders. Then he was bending to
seize Kerry by the arms and pull her to her feet. 'Are
you OK?'

She nodded, neither daring nor caring to look at him
directly. 'Just muddy,' she murmured huskily.

'A shower will take care of that,' he said. 'Go and get
your things. I'll stand guard while you take it.'

She went because there seemed no other course at the
moment but to do as he said. He escorted her across to
the shower-house without saying a word—and without
touching her again.

'Save it,' he advised when she attempted to speak.
'We'll talk after you're through.'

There was mud in her hair. She shampooed it out,
rinsing until it was squeaky clean. She was just putting
off the moment when Brad got round to saying the obvious, she acknowledged unhappily, reaching for her
towel. Damn Pete Lomas for underlining the vulner-
ability she had fought so hard to disprove. Whenever
there were people like him her position was never going
to be secure.

Brad was waiting for her when she got outside again.
There was plenty of noise coming from the rec., but the
compound was deserted.

'You don't need to say it,' she got out as he fell into step at her side. 'I've had just about enough myself. There's a flight out on Thursday morning, isn't there? If someone will run me down early enough, I'll take it.'

His glance was appraising. 'Does that mean you're giving up on the whole idea?'

Her chin lifted, her spirit reasserting itself. 'Not necessarily. I've just had enough of this place, that's all.' She paused. 'What are you going to do about Pete Lomas?'

There was no change in his expression. 'Do you want me to fire him?'

She thought about it for a moment, then sighed, 'No. In some ways he was right. I *was* asking for it. There has to be a better way of handling even his type.'

'Staying away from them is probably the easiest.'

'I can't spend the rest of my life avoiding the problems.'

'You don't have to go out looking for them, either.'

The sigh came again. 'Brad, it's no use. Whatever happens, I'm not settling for anything less. Others can do the surveys and site investigations and economic appraisals, et cetera, but this is where it's all at.'

'Concrete results?' His tone was ironic. 'If you feel so strongly about it, why leave now?'

They had reached his room door. Hair already drying to a red-gold cloud about her face, she lifted clear green eyes. 'I think you know why,' she said. 'Goodnight, Brad.'

She had gained her own room and was about to close the door when he pushed his way through. The glitter was there again in his eyes, but different somehow. Kerry felt herself start to tremble as he took hold of her—felt the world shake as his lips found hers in a kiss that had no anger in it, no design to hurt, just an overwhelming passion and a promise of things to come.

They made love right there on the narrow bed. And this time there was an unaccustomed tenderness in the strong features when he at last lifted his head to look at her.

'If I can't talk sense into you,' he growled softly, 'it looks like I'll have to find a way of keeping an eye on you!'

'How?' she whispered.

'We'll work it out. KDC will be tendering for the Nigerian job. That would be a start.'

Kerry brought up a hand to trace the firm line of his mouth, still not sure of his meaning. 'Start of what?'

'The only man-and-wife team in the business—that I know of, at any rate.' He caught her fingertip between his teeth, biting on it gently. 'I've tried every which way to get you out from under my skin, green eyes, but you just wouldn't get. I only hope you meant it when you said you loved me, because I don't intend letting you off the hook now, believe me!'

She could feel the warmth curling through her again, the heady delight and relief of hearing him say what she had longed to hear him say. 'I meant it,' she said huskily. 'I never meant anything more. Oh, Brad, if you only knew what I've been going through this last three weeks...'

'No more than I've gone through myself. One look at you on that plane, and it all came flooding back. I fell hook, line and sinker for an eighteen-year-old girl four years ago, and I couldn't have her. It was the thought of going through *that* again that I couldn't stand.'

'I'm sorry about Careen,' Kerry offered, and saw him smile.

'You'll be able to do your explaining to her personally, now. She'll still blame me, of course. Probably rightly so. You were ripe for romance, and I took advantage of it. I should have left you alone after that lunchtime.'

'If you had we might never have got together at all,' she pointed out. 'And that would have been a real pity, don't you think?' Her voice thickened as emotion swept her. 'Oh, God, I love you!'

He dropped his head to kiss her breast. 'No more than I love you,' he said against her skin. 'It isn't always going to be easy finding ways to be together, but we'll manage. The next couple of years will be more or less taken care of, anyway.'

Her laugh came soft and low. 'You're mighty confident of that contract!'

'As you said,' he came back imperturbably, 'your father will always take KDC when it comes to dam building. We should have time to fit in a wedding and a honeymoon before it gets under way, wouldn't you say?'

'Plenty.' She laughed again. 'I don't know what Dad's going to say. I lose two Land Rovers and find a husband, all in a few weeks. Not exactly what he had in mind when he sent me out here, for sure.'

'He'll get over it. He may even have a suspicion that the phone call I made was rather more than simple altruism. No matter what,' Brad added with satisfying certainty, 'you and I are going to be married.' There was a pause, and then a slight change of tone. 'Just one thing. I think it would still be a good idea if you left this job.

I'll miss you like crazy, but it's either that or a whole lot of frustration—to say nothing of keeping a tight rein on Lomas and his ilk.' He studied her face in the shaft of moonlight striking in through the window, his own features clearly defined. 'It's only a matter of two or three weeks. How do you feel about it?'

'Terrible,' she confessed ruefully, 'but I do see the sense.' She lifted herself to press her lips into the tight whorls of hair on his chest, running both hands lightly down over the tautly muscled body to his sharp intake of breath. 'I want you,' she whispered with urgency. 'At least we can have tonight.'

'You've got me,' he said, lips claiming hers. 'Not just tonight, but for life.'

H A R L E Q U I N
American Romance®

THE ROMANCE THAT STARTED IT ALL!

For Diane Bauer and Nick Granatelli, the walk down the aisle was a rocky road....

Don't miss the romantic prequel to WITH THIS RING—

I THEE WED
BY ANNE McALLISTER

Harlequin American Romance #387

Let Anne McAllister take you to Cambridge, Massachusetts, to the night when an innocent blind date brought a reluctant Diane Bauer and Nick Granatelli together. For Diane, a smoldering attraction like theirs had only one fate, one future—marriage. The hard part, she learned, was convincing her intended....

Watch for Anne McAllister's I THEE WED, available *now* from Harlequin American Romance.

ITW

If you loved American Romance #387
I THEE WED . . .

You are cordially invited to attend the
wedding of Diane Bauer and
Nick Granatelli. . . .

**ONE WEDDING—FOUR LOVE STORIES
FROM YOUR FAVORITE HARLEQUIN
AUTHORS!**

BETHANY CAMPBELL
BARBARA DELINSKY
BOBBY HUTCHINSON
ANN McALLISTER

*The church is booked, the reception arranged and the
invitations mailed. All Diane and Nick have to do is walk
down the aisle. Little do they realize that the most cherished
day of their lives will spark so many romantic notions. . . .*

Available wherever Harlequin books are sold.   HW3

H A R L E Q U I N
American Romance®

RELIVE THE MEMORIES....

All the way from turn-of-the-century Ellis Island to the future of the '90s...**A CENTURY OF AMERICAN ROMANCE** takes you on a nostalgic journey through the twentieth century.

Watch for all the **A CENTURY OF AMERICAN ROMANCE** titles coming to you one per month over the next two months in Harlequin American Romance, including #385 MY ONLY ONE by Eileen Nauman, in April.

Don't miss a day of **A CENTURY OF AMERICAN ROMANCE**.

A CENTURY OF
AMERICAN ROMANCE

1980s

The women...the men...the passions...the memories....